AS A GANGLY, SKINNY
LITTLE THIRTEEN-YEAR-OLD, HICCUP
HORRENDOUS HADDOCK THE THIRD ISN'T
THE MOST OBVIOUS-LOOKING HERO.

But a Hero he is and now he must
prove himself again, because the
DRAGON REBELLION is coming!
DO-O-O-O-OM!

Or is it? According to Alvin the Treacherous's
witch of a mother, every man, woman and child
is done for. Unless of course, a new King of the
Wilderwest can be found.

WHO could the new King possibly be?
The signs are pointing to Hiccup, but **GOODNESS
GRACIOUS!** Alvin the Treacherous will do
everything in his power to be crowned King . . .

You don't **HAVE** to read the Hiccup books in order.
But if you want to, this is the right order:

1. How to train your Dragon
2. How to be a Pirate
3. How to speak Dragonese
4. How to Cheat a Dragon's Curse
5. How to Twist a Dragon's Tale
6. A Hero's Guide to Deadly Dragons
7. How to Ride a Dragon's Storm
8. How to Break a Dragon's Heart
9. How to Steal a Dragon's Sword
10. How to Seize a Dragon's Jewel
11. How to Betray a Dragon's Hero
12. How to Fight a Dragon's Fury

JOIN HICCUP ON HIS QUEST

(although he doesn't quite realise he is on one yet...)

THE PROPHECY OF

THE KING'S LOST THINGS

'The Dragontime is coming
And only a King can save you now.
The King shall be the
Champion of Champions.

You shall know the King
By the King's Lost Things.
A fang-free dragon, my second-best sword,
My Roman shield,
An arrow-from-the-land-that-does-not-exist,
The heart's stone, the key-that-opens-all-locks,
The ticking-thing, the Throne, the Crown.

And last and best of all the ten,
The Dragon Jewel shall save all men.'

Hiccup Horrendous Haddock the Third

Hiccup's hunting dragon, Toothless

Camicazi

Fishlegs

Horrorcow

The Witch Excellinor a particularly unpleasant and scary witch

FLASHBURN

STOICK the VAST
Hiccup's father, the
Chief of the Hooligan Tribe

Alvin
the
Treacherous

Snotface
Snotlout

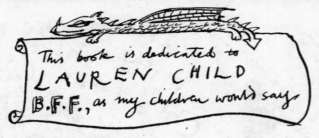

This book is dedicated to
LAUREN CHILD
B.F.F., as my children would say

HODDER CHILDREN'S BOOKS

First published in Great Britain in 2011 by Hodder & Stoughton
This edition published in 2017 by Hodder & Stoughton

5 7 9 10 8 6

SPECIAL EDITON

A CIP catalogue record for this book is available from the British Library.

ISBN: 978-1-444-94189-0

Cover design by Jennifer Stephenson
Background cover illustration by Christopher Gibbs

Printed and bound by Clays Ltd, St Ives Plc

The paper and board used in this book are made from wood from responsible sources.

Hodder Children's Books
An imprint of Hachette Children's Group, Part of Hodder & Stoughton
Carmelite House, 50 Victoria Embankment, London EC4Y 0DZ
An Hachette UK Company
www.hachette.co.uk

THANKYOU to Simon Cowell, Anne McNeil, Naomi Potterman, Alison Still, Jennifer Stephenson, and Judit Komar for your help in creating this book.

How to Steal a Dragon's Sword

written and illustrated by
CRESSIDA COWELL

Hodder
Children's
Books

A division of Hachette Children's Group

TOOTHLESS, Hiccup's
small disobedient dragon

~ CONTENTS ~

THE DRAGON'S NOSE
THE HAUNTED MARSHES
The Gorge of the Thunderbolt of Thor
ARCHIPELAGO
Peaceable Country
The Island of the Quiet Life
Flashburn's School of Swordfighting
The Summer Current
Berserk
BLOODSPILT BAY
Dragon Hatching Grounds
THE MYSTERY
THE WATERLANDS

A small plea to readers:

PLEASE DO NOT BLAME THE STORY

Up until now Hiccup has just been playing at adventure, learning to be a Hero when the stakes are not so high. But darker and more difficult times are coming now to the Isle of Berk.

Please do not blame the story.
The story cannot help itself. For sometimes, we do not realize it at the time, but the story we are all a part of is not just a story about Vikings and islands and dragons.
It is a story about growing up.
And one of the things about growing up, one of the inescapable, inevitable laws, is that one day...
One day... One day...

It is going to happen.

I am sorry, but it's true.

PROLOGUE BY HICCUP HORRENDOUS HADDOCK III THE LAST OF THE GREAT VIKING HEROES

Now that I am an old, old man, the past seems very far away.

But once there were dragons in the Archipelago.

And once I was a boy, a boy who in the thirteenth year of my life made a terrible mistake.

I released the Dragon Furious from the prison of Berserk.

The dragon promised to fly into exile in the icy wastes of the north for one year only. One year's grace, and then he vowed that he would bring down a Dragon Rebellion whose only aim was the absolute and utter extinction of the entire human race.

Over the next year the boy-that-once-was-me grew like a weed, at least three inches taller. My arms were sticking right out of my shirtsleeves, but the year came and went, with no sign of the Dragon Furious, or of his Rebellion.

I heaved a sigh of relief, and began to hope that

perhaps the terrible hurts of a hundred years of imprisonment had been soothed by the chill of those innocent snows, and diving free and joyous through the pin-sharp cold waters, chasing the fleeting seals in that endless chilly wilderness, the dragon had returned to the happy carefree life of his ancestors.

Perhaps he had remembered himself up there in his element, and what if he had forgotten his promise, and maybe he might not return after all?

Perhaps.

What if?

Maybe.

But in the quiet watches of the night, the words of the Dragon Furious came hissing and burning back into my brain, and they were not words that melted like water into snow-drops. They were words of flame, and they hissed and leapt into burning, terrible life in my dreams.

'We shall scourge this world with fire, and leave no wretched human being alive, not a single one. For over the last hundred years I have been looking into the past and into the future, and I tell you this, Boy... humans and dragons cannot live together...'

The words spat through my brain like living, burning snakes:

'... and so I will call the dragons from far and wide, from the depths of the ocean and the ends of the earth, and we shall fight the final battle before it is too late.'

'NO!' I shrieked in my dream. 'NO! NO! NO! NO! NO!'

But time cannot tick backwards. The boy-that-once-was-me could not stop it.

And the Dragon was coming.

1. THE GREATEST DAY OF YOUR LIFE (NOT)

One long-ago winter's midnight, Hiccup Horrendous Haddock the Third awoke with a frightened start.

Despite being the Hope and Heir to the Tribe of the Hairy Hooligans, Hiccup was a gangly, skinny, ordinary-looking boy, with the kind of face that was easy to overlook in a crowd.

To tell the truth, he had not been sleeping very well.

It is difficult to sleep well if one's bed is a hammock suspended three quarters of the way up the Hard Way of Angry Mountain.

The Hard Way of Angry Mountain is a cliff so high that it takes two days and a night to climb it. It is so vertical that a climber has to hammer in a couple of nails and spend that night sleeping uneasily in a hammock hung precariously from the shiny rock.

Hiccup's riding-dragon, the Windwalker, sleeping on a little shelf of rock a couple of feet away, was supposed to be looking out for danger.

However it was still winter, the Windwalker's

hibernation time, so he was barely even awake in the daytime, and now that it was night he was sleeping so soundly he might as well have been dead. His long, untidy body sprawled messily on the ledge, snoring as loud as a cow with a cold.

Anything dangerous would have had to come right up and sit on his head before he'd take any notice whatsoever.

Toothless, Hiccup's tiny, selfish Common or Garden hunting-dragon, had not noticed anything either. He was fast asleep on Hiccup's chest, sending out smoke rings that filled the hammock.

But it was danger that woke Hiccup up.

He was sure of it.

Hiccup's heart was pumping like a jack-in-a-box, and he was suddenly, wildly awake, for with every fibre of his being he sensed danger.

Danger all around him.

Frankly, they should have been safe enough, high up on a cliff-face, in the middle of the wintertime, when most of the dangerous dragons in the Archipelago were still hibernating.

The only danger should have been if the hammock fell down.

So why did Hiccup's heart tick so quick, and why was his stomach so faint that he was nearly sick?

Moving very slowly (he didn't want to dislodge himself), Hiccup peered over the edge of the hammock.

The bottom of the cliff was sickeningly far below. Hiccup swallowed, and tried not to look down.

They were so far up he could see for miles in every direction, as if he were looking down on a map of the Archipelago. To the west, the sea. To the north, the sinister jagged gash of the Gorge of the Thunderbolt of Thor. Further north still, the drifting icebergs and ragged peaks of the Cold Mountains.

And here, right here, the strange mainland landscape of ice and snow, relieved by weirdly warm bubbling pools, belching drifting smoke upwards like dragons snoring.

A couple of feet away on the cliff hung the patched hammock of Hiccup's best friend Fishlegs.

Fishlegs,
too, was snoring,
but that was probably
his asthma. (Fishlegs
was unfortunately
allergic to his own dragon,
Horrorcow, who was in
there with him.) Or it could
have been his hay fever.
(Fishlegs was the only person
Hiccup knew who could get
hay fever in the middle of the
winter.)

And above, way above,
was the night sky, brilliantly

studded with stars.

The sky was full of noises. Sounds more eerie than thunder, stranger than lightning.

A high-pitched sound that made the eardrums throb, like whales calling to each other in an alien universe.

And up there in the sky, Hiccup could see advancing black shadowy shapes, slowly flying towards them over the Gorge of the Thunderbolt of Thor.

They were too far away for him to identify which types of dragon they were exactly, but there was something nightmarish about their wings, and he knew them deep in his soul.

When a young rabbit spots a hawk circling above, it may never have seen such a creature before – but there is some ancestral memory that tells it to be afraid, to leap in great panicky bounds to the safety of the burrow. So it was with these dragons.

It was not, of course, that Hiccup had never seen dragons before.

He lived in a world full of the creatures, both wild and domesticated.

But what was different about these dragons was their behaviour. They were a number of different species, and they were acting as if they were in a hunting party. And dragon species did not generally join together to hunt humans.

Maybe they had done, once, long ago.

But for as long as the old ones could remember, they did not hunt humans.

A wild dragon would eat you, of course, if you

26

happened to cross its path and it was hungry. But there was no organized hunting of the human, as perhaps there had been way in the past.

Hiccup's scalp prickled all over with fear as if he were being climbed all over by black beetles. He strained so hard to hear into that blackness that it was as if his ears were growing outwards. And somehow above the roar of the wind he could just hear a truly terrifying noise, a savage hiss in Dragonese, but nastier than he had ever heard Dragonese spoken, it was so cold with hatred.

There was something scarily trance-like about the way the words were spat out, so faint he could hardly catch them. But perhaps it was better if he could not hear them after all:

'MAKE RED your claws
with HUMAN BLOOD...
OBLITERATE the HUMAN FILTH...
Torch the humans like a wood
The Rebellion is coming...'

Closer, closer, flew the advancing dragons, heading straight for the cliff where the hammocks perched.

Hiccup craned his neck even further upwards. About sixty feet above him were the hammocks of the other young Warriors of the Tribes of the Archipelago, hammered into the cliff, just like his own. They were a half an hour's climbing ahead of Fishlegs and Hiccup, and while Fishlegs's and Hiccup's hammocks were made out of brown patched blankets, theirs were made out of old ships' sails. The gaudy patterns of these sails, such as red and white stripes, or blue and gold diamonds, made them stick out against the cliff like a flamingo sitting in a bog.

The mysterious dragons were heading straight for them.

Hiccup could see what they were now. He recognized them from their wing patterns.

They were a mixture of some of the nastiest types of dragons in the Archipelago: Razorwings and Tonguetwisters and Doldrums and Vampire Ghouldeaths.

I've got to warn the others, thought Hiccup, and he opened his mouth to shout, but terror seemed to

have strangled
his vocal cords,
like it does in
your worst
nightmares.

'Squeak,'
panted
Hiccup
faintly, 'squeak
squeak squeak…'

That wasn't
going to do much
good.

And then:
'Dragons…'
And as an
afterthought,
'Really nasty ones.'

This wasn't
even waking up
Toothless, let alone the young warriors
snoring peacefully, unawares, high
above him.

The dragons were horribly near

now, flying in close formation – most unnatural
behaviour for dragons. They were drawing down their
legs and stretching out their talons, ready to strike.
The Warriors were totally helpless, they'd be killed
inside their gaudy cocoons as they slept.

Hiccup leant across to the small ledge in the
cliff where he had stowed his rucksack. Hands
shaking, he drew out his bow and an arrow from the
quiver.

Perhaps it was lucky that Hiccup was so far away.
If he could see what the leader of the dragon pack was
doing now… he might have fainted.

For the leader was a Tonguetwister dragon.

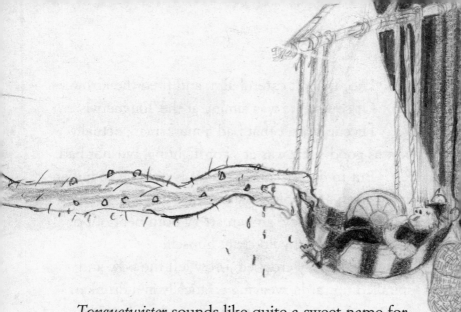

Tonguetwister sounds like quite a sweet name for a dragon. But I am afraid that Tonguetwisters remove the limbs from their victims so that they can no longer run away.

I'm sorry, but it's true.

Hovering perfectly still next to one of the hammocks, the Tonguetwister slowly opened its mouth and out flicked its tongue: a tongue thicker than a man's muscly arm. The forked ends of that tongue were flexible and delicate.

The tongue slid inside one of the hammocks, the one belonging to Hiccup's unpleasant cousin Snotlout, and rummaged around as if looking for something.

Hiccup took careful aim, and fired the arrow.

Of course, he was aiming at the Tonguetwister.

Hiccup wasn't that bad a marksman, actually. Not as good as he was at swordfighting, but not bad.

But to do Hiccup justice, it is difficult to fire an arrow from a wobbling hammock. Particularly when you are using a bow and an arrow both bent out of shape, ironically, by Snotlout himself.

The slightly-crooked arrow left the bow and spiralled upwards, weaving erratically in a drunken fashion. At the last minute it plunged to the right, missed the dragon entirely, and sank into Snotlout's left calf.

It wasn't quite what Hiccup had intended, but it did have the desired effect... sort of.

Snotlout let out a small, muffled scream, as you would, of course, if you had just been shot in the leg by an arrow, and leapt out of the hammock... much to the surprise (and annoyance) of the Tonguetwister, who hadn't yet got hold of one of Snotlout's limbs.

Of course, in his half-asleep, arrow-ridden state, Snotlout had completely forgotten he was three-quarters of the way up a cliff. Down he plunged, hurtling down that hysterical drop, past the hammocks

HELP ME YOU IDIOT!

of his fellow-
Warriors, and past
Hiccup himself, who
reached out desperately to
try and catch him, though
Snotlout would have been
far too heavy…

And that would
have been the end of
Snotlout if there had not been
a tree growing out of the cliff-
face not far below Hiccup. The tree
broke Snotlout's fall, and though he carried on
downwards, he ju-u-ust managed to grab hold of one
of the lower bendy branches to save himself.

So there was Snotlout, dangling from the tree, a
three-thousand-foot drop below him, so surprised, that
he, too, could not make a sound, staring up at Hiccup
with round, terrified eyes.

'HELP ME, YOU IDIOT,' mouthed Snotlout
gracelessly. Snotlout was not one for being polite, even
when he had just been saved from a nasty fate at the
tongue of a Tonguetwister, and was still depending on
the person he was insulting to save his life.

He couldn't hold on for long, but was slightly out of Hiccup's reach.

Hiccup frantically scrabbled around in his hammock, trying to get out one of his climbing-ropes so that Snotlout could grab on to it. But even at the best of times, manoeuvring inside a hammock is like trying to put your underpants on inside a pillowcase, and in this instance, with the hammock fugged up with Toothless's smoke, it was like taking part in some bizarre sauna-like sweating ceremony.

Back and forth Hiccup struggled and swayed but he couldn't find the end of the beastly climbing-rope and his hands were slippery with perspiration. He gave a frantic wriggle like a stranded worm... and accidentally drew his sword instead of pulling out the climbing-rope...

With a dreadful ripping sound, the sword cut the old faded brown hammock right in half.

'Wooooooooaaaaahhhh!'

Now, at last, he could find his voice.

'DRAGON ATTAAACKKKKK!!!!!!'

It was an enormous shout, the full terrified blast of Hiccup's lungs echoing off the dark walls of the cliff, sending the shout back again, and on and up.

A couple of feet away, Fishlegs caught the full blast of the shout, and rocketed into wakefulness like an exploding starfish. He very nearly fell out of his hammock as well. Way, way up the cliff, every hammock wobbled and wiggled as its occupants blearily sat up blurting, 'Wossat? Wossgoingon?'

'E-e-e-e-k!' squealed Toothless in alarm, opening his eyes and putting out his wings as he realized he was plummeting towards the ground.

The dragons paused in their
attack, hovering for a moment in the cold night
air. They adjusted the lights in their yellow eyes (an
extraordinary trick that some dragons possess) from a
slight glow to a dazzling glare and turned their heads
downward...

And pinpointed Hiccup, swinging on his
hammock remains, illuminating him in the dazzling
brightness of their many searchlight eyebeams, so that
he shone in brilliant detail against the darkness of the
cliff.

'Uh oh... WINDWALKER! WAKE UP!!!!'
yelled Hiccup, waving his sword around wildly. (He
yelled this in Dragonese, for Hiccup was one of the

few Vikings, before or since, who could speak this fascinating language.)

'Hoooooonnnnnng... sshuuuuunh...' snored the Windwalker.

The swarm of dragons, eerily still hanging way above Hiccup, hissed with slow, chilling anger. Something in their eyes clicked. It was the little focus lid, a shutter that came down over their eyes and enabled them to see objects pin sharp from an extraordinary distance.

They hung there for a moment more without moving.

Only their eyes shifted a little, following the waving of Hiccup's sword.

And then they folded back their wings and dived.

The Prey Dive.

What a beautiful sight, if Hiccup had only been in the state of mind to appreciate it! It's a shame that he was hanging by only one blanket strand off the highest cliff in the Archipelago at the time.

For the Prey Dive is a glorious feat of aerial acrobatics, where the dragon goes into freefall with his wings folded back. And to see a swarm of gigantic dragons performing this simultaneously, so vertically and so close to the Hard Way of Angry Mountain, that their wings were practically skimming the cliff itself, in the dead of night-time – well, I can tell you, that should have been a privilege and a pleasure, the kind of sight to see before you die. (And frankly, if you see this kind of sight, the likelihood is you're going to die pretty soon anyway.)

The lead dragon opened his jaws, as the dragons came screaming down at Hiccup, who made a final wild wriggling swing back on to the cliff at the last minute, and the entire swarm of dragons missed him and carried on, unable to stop, in their brilliant dive down the cliff.

Hiccup scrabbled around wildly, desperately
trying to get a foothold on the glass-smooth rock face.
He could feel his fingers sliding slightly down what
was left of the hammock. He couldn't hold on much
longer... but there was nothing for his feet to grip on
to, and he swung out again over the
dizzying drop.

Meanwhile, Toothless was
bouncing up and down on
the Windwalker's stomach,
desperately trying to get him
to wake up. 'W-W-Wake
up! Wake up! Or Toothless'll
grind your bones into broth!'
yelled the little dragon.

'Wake up you lolloping l-l-
lazybones l-l-loser!'

'Hooooooooooooong...
ssshuuuuuuuh...' The
Windwalker's snores were happier
and more contented than ever. In his
dreams he was flitting happily from tree to
tree and a dear little butterfly was gently tickling his
stomach with its dear little butterfly wings.

39

Fishlegs tried to get himself out of his hammock to help but his foot got stuck in one of the ropes.

Clang!

The fiftieth dragon, another Tonguetwister, having screeched past Hiccup at one hundred and fifty miles an hour, did a lightning last-minute breakneck turn, gripping on to the cliff with the hooks on the ends of its wings.

Brilliant. Absolutely brilliant flying skills.

With eyes firmly set on Hiccup, the Tonguetwister rapidly began to haul itself by its wings across the cliff towards the dangling and seemingly helpless Hiccup.

Toothless had given up bouncing on the Windwalker's stomach and was now heaving with all his tiny strength, trying to nudge the happily snoring Windwalker off the ledge in the hope that that would bring him to his senses.

'Oh, don't go, dear little butterfly,' whispered the Windwalker in his dreams, blowing reproachful crooning smoke rings, 'stay with me, little fluttery one, and we'll dance the flower dance together...'

'HICCUP, YOU FOOL!' shouted Snotlout, hanging on by his hands to the tree a couple of feet below. 'DO SOMETHING, FOR ONCE IN YOUR LIFE! I CAN'T HOLD ON MUCH LONGER!'

But Hiccup had problems of his own.

'Aaaaieeeeee!' screeched Hiccup, as the Tonguetwister crawled, bat-like, ever closer, and as it opened its mouth he could see the dreadful, muscly, hairy tongue lurking slug-like in the depths.

The dragon's alligator jaws snapped open, and its horrible tongue snaked out and around Hiccup's sword, dragging Hiccup's left hand with it, off the rope…

The dragon shifted its grip a moment and shivering with revulsion, Hiccup felt the tongue curling around his whole arm.

Ping!

Another strand of the blanket broke, leaving him dangling by only the tiniest threads above the drop.

The dragon paused, preparing to twist off Hiccup's arm with the sword…

2. WHY THEY WERE THERE IN THE FIRST PLACE

I'll take a little breather while the dragon pauses, just to recap on what had brought Hiccup into this situation in the first place.

It's always very irritating when you get hurtled into the middle of a story without any explanation as to why the heroes got there, and how they got there, and what on earth they were doing camping three quarters of the way up the Hard Way of Angry Mountain in the middle of the winter in the first place.

It was a perfectly barmy idea, surely?

Here is what happened.

Bright and early that morning, the Tribes of the Archipelago had gathered at the foot of Angry Mountain, in a great noisy jostling crowd of tents and sledges and skis, greeting old friends and enemies with a bump of their massive bellies, hunting-dragons wheeling above them in the air, riding-dragons getting into dragon fights.

Perched right on the top of Angry Mountain was Flashburn's School of Swordfighting. The Tribes were

tick tock tick
tock tick

travelling there for the annual three-week celebration of feasting, fighting and festivities, which ended on New Year's Day with a swordfighting competition and the New Year, New Warrior Ceremony, in which youngsters across the Archipelago finally crossed over from childhood into adulthood, and became Warriors of their Tribes.

There are two ways to climb Angry Mountain.

There is the Easy Way, a gentle, pleasant incline that you can stroll up quite merrily without even getting out of breath. That is the way the adult Warriors would take, with their sledges and tents and riding-dragons and Driver Dragons and weapons and provisions.

And then there is the Hard Way, a sheer vertical cliff-face of rock that takes two days to climb. That is the way the young Warriors-to-Be would take, to prove their worthiness to be admitted into the Tribes.*

The Warriors-to-Be were looking up at the gigantic rock face rather dubiously.

They were a motley crew of pimply adolescents, all of them much larger and more muscly than Hiccup and Fishlegs. (Apart from Camicazi, who was a good friend of Hiccup's: a tiny, fierce little Bog-Burglar with

---

* The test had first been set way in the distant and dangerous past when Vikings did not have riding-dragons to aid them. So the rule was, the cliff must be climbed without dragonly assistance.

a great deal of blonde
hair that looked
as if she had
carelessly
combed it with
a pitch-fork.)

Gobber
the Belch,
teacher in charge of the
Hooligan Pirate Training
Programme, was giving
the Warriors-to-Be a quick
pep talk.

Camicazi
(a tiny fierce little
Bog-Burglar)

Gobber was a six-and-a-half-foot man-mountain
with lungs like a fog-horn and ears like deformed
cauliflowers. He didn't have a sensitive side.

'OK, Warriors, listen up!' he shouted. 'This is a
stroll in the park! All you have to do is spend the next
day and night climbing this sheer vertical cliff-face.
Once we get to the school, you will be practising
for the swordfighting competition on New Year's
Day. This is your chance to learn and get tips from
the greatest swordfighter in the Archipelago,
Flashburn himself!'

Ooohs and *aaahs* from the Warriors-to-Be.

'Oh, I can't wait to meet Flashburn in real life,' Camicazi chatted excitedly to Hiccup and Fishlegs. 'He's supposed to be the perfect Hero…'

'Here he co-o-o-omes!' called out Thuggory the Meathead, pointing upward.

A gorgeous Red Tiger dragon, with Flashburn crouched very low on its back, dived down out of nowhere from above. Camicazi let out a 'Wow!' and punched the air as the dragon zoomed over their heads, so low that they could feel the wind of its wings.

The dragon swooped so very low that Flashburn leant over and very cheekily grabbed Stoick the Vast's helmet off his head before flying upwards again.

Stoick the Vast, Hiccup's father, was built in the traditional Viking mould, with muscles like footballs, a beard like a thunderstorm, and about as many brain cells as would fit into a teeny tiny teaspoon.

He was not amused.

'Oh, that Flashburn, he hasn't changed one bit!' snorted Stoick as everybody laughed and the youngsters *ooohed* and *aaahed*.

'COME DOWN, YOU SHOW-OFF!' yelled

FLASHBURN ↗

I am the
GREATEST....

(The Hero with a Healthy
sense of Self-Respect)

Stoick. 'IT'S GOING TO BE NIGHTFALL BY THE
TIME WE GET GOING AT THIS RATE! I don't
know. These Heroes. No consideration...'

Finally with a graceful, zooming swoop,
Flashburn's Red Tiger came in to land directly in
front of Stoick and Flashburn did a complete double
somersault over the dragon's head, landed on his feet,
and offered Stoick back his helmet with an elegant
bow.

'There you are, Stoick, my dear...'

'DON'T CALL ME DEAR!' fumed Stoick,
snatching it back. 'GET ON WITH IT, WHY DON'T
YOU?'

Flashburn smiled, and sprang on to a nearby rock
so that everyone could see him.

Flashburn was an extremely good-looking man
with a lot of long blond hair.

His famous gold swordfighting belt was around
his waist, with the captured swords of some of the
most famous swordfighters in the Archipelago thrust
into it.

'Greetings, Old Fatsos!' smiled Flashburn
good-humouredly. 'Why, Mogadon the Meathead,
you've put on weight, I hardly recognized you. Bertha,

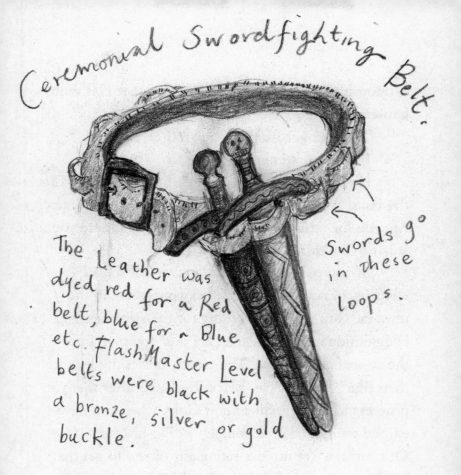

Ceremonial Swordfighting Belt.

The Leather was dyed red for a Red belt, blue for a Blue etc. FlashMaster Level belts were black with a bronze, silver or gold buckle.

Swords go in these loops.

I'm not sure that shade of violet really suits you. Madguts the Murderous you're losing your hair *already…*

'Greetings, Warriors-to-Be!' Flashburn ignored the slight rumblings of annoyance from the older Warriors. 'I have the great good luck and the extraordinary good fortune to be the Great Flashburn himself. You may cheer now.'

The younger Warriors cheered.

Flashburn seemed to expect it.

He pointed at the vertical cliff-face of rock. 'This, the Hard Way up Angry Mountain, is the ultimate test. Are you the stuff that a Hero is made of? Or are you a jellyfish in a skirt?

'If you pass this test, and get to MY school, which is, of course, the most brilliant school in the universe, you will be practising for the swordfighting competition on New Year's Day, and competing for the swordfighting belts. The Green Belt is the lowest, then Blue, then Purple, Black, Red, and after that you progress to Bronze, Silver and Gold, when you have earned the right to call yourself a "FlashMaster".*
Of course, we're not expecting any of *you* to get that far. There are not that many FlashMasters in the Archipelago. You never made FlashMaster Level, did you now, Murderous, my dear?'

Madguts the Murderous gave a furious strangled grunt. 'No finesse,' explained Flashburn kindly. 'The Murderous fight like pigs in pyjamas.'

Madguts gave a dreadful roar and charged at

---

* You only get a Gold Belt if you beat another Gold FlashMaster.

Flashburn, sword drawn.

Flashburn did not bother to draw one of the many swords thrust into his swordfighting belt. Instead, he reached into the nearest rucksack and took out… a spoon and an apple.

This seemed to enrage Madguts even further.

Madguts lunged forward like an infuriated bull, and Flashburn's spoon and Madguts's sword met in a bewildering flurry of metal feints and parries.

To the delight of the cheering Tribesmen, ten seconds later, Madguts found himself flat on his back in the snow, with an apple stuck on the end of his sword and a spoon on the end of his nose.

'You see? No finesse. And dead as a dodo in less than ten seconds,' grinned Flashburn, bowing to the applause. 'And I wouldn't laugh too hard, nobody here could have lasted any longer. Thus endeth the First Lesson, Warriors-in-Waiting.

'Cheerio,' he cried, springing on to his Red Tiger with a perfect, god-like vault, winking at the women and waving his sword in goodbye. 'And good luck! We'll have the banquet ready when you get there! Remember, there is nothing wrong with a healthy sense of self-respect, especially when you're as

51

brilliant as I am!'

'He's so cool, isn't he?' sighed Camicazi.

'As you said,' purred Stormfly, Camicazi's
beautiful golden hunting-dragon, batting her eyelashes,
'he is the perfect Hero...'

'He's n-n-not so perfect,' grumbled Toothless,
who was smitten with Stormfly. 'Even for a human,
he's got a big nose.'

They had come, at last, to the Parting of the
Ways.

With much hearty patting on backs, and cheery
waves, the adults of the Tribe marched off to go the
Easy Way, on their skis and skates and with their Driver
Dragons pulling sledges.

And the Warriors-to-Be began to fasten on their
gigantic rucksacks for the long climb up the Hard Way.

'We'll beat you to the top!' grinned Camicazi,
running to join her gang of Bog-Burglars, a terrifying
gaggle of female bodybuilders, 'because girls are better
than boys and always will be!'

Stoick the Vast bustled up to wish Hiccup
goodbye.

'Good luck, Hiccup my boy! No pressure, but
remember: *I* became a Gold FlashMaster when I was

only eighteen, and so I'm expecting great things from you, Hiccup, great things. Signs of leadership and so forth. This is your chance to impress your peer group in the other Tribes!'

'Great,' said Hiccup gloomily. 'No pressure, then.'

Stoick stomped off happily, and Old Wrinkly, Hiccup's grandfather, hobbled forward.

There was an expression of slight horror in Old Wrinkly's old whelk eyes, a tremble to his ancient limbs.

'I have a dreadful foreboding that terrible danger awaits you at the Flashburn School of Swordfighting, Hiccup,' muttered Old Wrinkly, holding up a skinny finger. 'The world will need a Hero, and it might as well be you. Keep your Things in tip-top condition, for they are the King's Things.' Old Wrinkly pointed at Hiccup's shabby collection of equipment. 'And remember, look after your sword, Hiccup, for it is the sword that points the way. Good luck!'

The old man shook Hiccup's hand as if he were shaking it for the last time, tears in his eyes, and with that, still muttering to himself, he hobbled off to join the elderly and the children, who would return to keep

Snotface
Snotlout

(Hiccup's
unpleasant
cousin)

the home fires burning on Berk.

'Great!' said Fishlegs, 'that's great, that is! *Terrible* danger, my favourite kind... and what was all that weird stuff about your Things being the King's Things?'

'I have no idea. The thing about grown-ups,' said Hiccup, trying to squeeze his blanket into his already bursting-at-the-seams rucksack, 'is that they're always wanting you to be this Great Hero and Leader. What's wrong with being NORMAL, for Thor's sake? What's wrong with just being SO-SO at stuff? They're just totally unrealistic...'

'Uh-oh...' said Fishlegs.

For at that moment reality was approaching in the form of someone who most definitely did *not* think Hiccup was a great Hero and Leader.

It was Snotface Snotlout, Hiccup's unpleasant first cousin, a large arrogant boy with the most enormous nostrils you have ever seen, closely followed by his sidekick Dogsbreath the Duhbrain.

'OK, listen up, Hooligans,' grinned Snotlout, addressing the thirteen or so Hooligan Warriors-to-Be, 'Hiccup will not be leading this group, because HE is not a leader. I am.'

'But Hiccup is the son of Stoick the Vast,' protested Fishlegs.

'*Who cares*,' grinned Snotlout, giving Fishlegs a painful kick in the shins, and a shove to Hiccup that was so violent it sent him sprawling on to the ground. 'Hiccup is scrawny and weedy and USELESS. He can't play Bashyball to save his life, his dragon is the size of a frog, and we can't be led by someone who has a friend like *you*.'

This was not a very kind thing to say, but admittedly Fishlegs was a little challenged in the Viking department. He was asthmatic, knock-kneed and nearly blind without his glasses. He was prone to hay fever, eczema, chilblains and chesty coughs.

He did have gifts of course. He was good at composing poetry, and he had a nice sarcastic sense of humour. But neither of these

Fishlegs (Hiccup's best friend)

skills were particularly prized in the Hooligan Tribe.

Snotlout drew his sword.

'With the Flashcut,' gloated Snotlout, making some lunges at imaginary opponents, 'I shall be the first Warrior-in-Training to make it to FlashMaster level. Trust me, I will. As for *you*,' purred Snotlout, 'maybe they should create new swordfighting belts for you two. How about yellow belts? Or pretty pink ones? That'd be good for a couple of cowards and their teeny-weeny little weapons.'

'Hur hur hur,' snorted Dogsbreath.

'HA HA HA HA!' laughed the Warriors-to-Be from some of the other, tougher Tribes – the Visithugs, the Bashem-Oiks and the Murderous – gathering round them as they sensed some fun was starting.

'Who are these pathetic weeds, Snotlout?' grinned Very Vicious the Visithug, a brute of a boy with a vigorous forest of hair sprouting from his ear-holes. 'Surely they can't be Hooligans?'

'They pretend to be,' sneered Snotlout.

Snotlout's eyes went as small and mean as a shark's.

He lunged at Hiccup's rucksack and rip, rip, rip went the Flashcut.

boing
boing

'Oh dear…' cooed Snotlout, holding up Hiccup's shredded hammock. 'My hand slipped… I seem to have caused a tiny little tear in your hammock. How will you make it the Hard Way up Angry Mountain when you haven't got anywhere to sleep? What a shame, you'll just have to stay awake for the whole night.'

'You big cheater, Snotlout!' replied Fishlegs hotly.

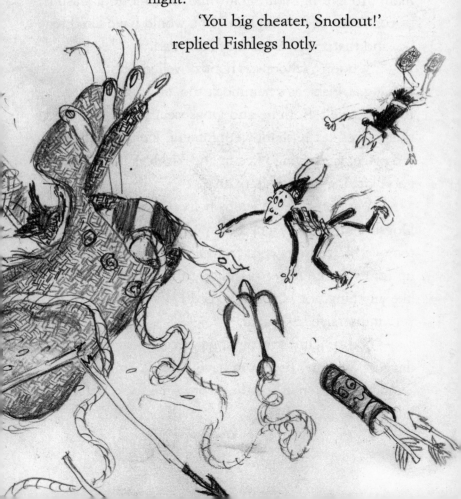

'You're just scared that if Hiccup makes it to the Flashburn School of Swordfighting, he's going to beat you!'

This really annoyed Snotlout.

The one thing that Hiccup was truly gifted at on the Pirate Training Programme was swordfighting. He hadn't fought Snotlout in a while, but Snotlout wasn't as confident of beating him as he would have liked to be, and that made Snotlout really mad.

'Whoops, whoops, whoops!' yelled Snotlout, lunging at Fishlegs's hammock too, and ripping that to bits as well. Both he and Dogsbreath then launched themselves at the shabby equipment, kicking it all over the place, and giving Hiccup and Fishlegs themselves a good kicking into the bargain.

A grinning Very Vicious helped them, and Dogsbreath held Hiccup down while Snotlout removed Hiccup's sword from his scabbard and held it up for everyone to see – and that made everyone laugh like anything, for Hiccup's sword Endeavour was not very impressive to look at.

'Your mighty sword, Chief Hiccup, or is it a dagger? Silly me, I seem to have bent it!' smiled Snotlout as he smashed the sword on a rock, before hurling it as far away as he could.

'Oh dear,' cooed Snotlout, 'how will you make Gold FlashMaster now?'

Well, the Hooligans and the Visithugs and the Bashem-Oiks and the Murderous were nearly sick, they thought that was so funny.

'Don't cwy, lickle ones,' lisped Snotlout, putting on a baby voice before he and Dogsbreath slouched off. 'You'll be better off with an excuse to stay here with the old people and the children...'

'COME ON, EVERYONE, FOLLOW ME!' yelled Snotlout. 'See you, LOSERS!'

And the rest of the grinning Warriors-to-Be began to climb the cliff after him, leaving Hiccup and Fishlegs bruised and sore and looking sadly at the wreckage of their belongings.

They were used to being humiliated by Snotlout in front of the other Hooligans, but this was worse, because it was in front of the other Tribes. It did not bode well for the three weeks they were going to spend at the Flashburn School of Swordfighting.

'You see?' sighed Hiccup, gloomily. 'The grown-ups have totally forgotten what it's like to be thirteen and have to deal with someone like Snotlout.'

Hiccup's sword had landed in a snowdrift some distance away and it was Toothless who found it (dragons are very good at sniffing out metal). It had indeed got a little bent in the process. Hiccup tried to bend it back again, but it was still a little skew-whiff.

All of his belongings had got similarly bashed up. There was a large dent in his shield, caused by the big fat foot of Dogsbreath the Duhbrain. The ticking thing was smashed and ticking wheezily, like it was out of breath. His bow was bent and most of his arrows were broken.

If these were indeed the King's Things, or whatever Old Wrinkly had been going on about, they were definitely NOT in tip-top condition *now*.

'How are we going to sleep if we don't have hammocks?' asked Fishlegs.

'We'll just have to make our blankets into hammocks,' said Hiccup.

And by the time they had done that, and collected their broken things which Snotlout and Dogsbreath had hurled all over the place, they were a good half an hour behind everyone else.

'Windwalker,' Hiccup said to his riding-dragon, 'you really ought to go round the Easy Way with everyone else.'

But Windwalker looked so saddened by this idea that Hiccup relented.

'Oh, OK then, I suppose as long as you don't actually HELP us climb up, that's fine, they didn't say you couldn't be here.'

'You spoil your dragons, you really do,' said Fishlegs as they began to climb the cliff.

'And we d-d-deserve it,' said Toothless.

All that day they climbed steadily up the cliff, with poor Fishlegs trying not to look down, because he was afraid of heights.

When night fell, they hammered in their nails and hung the brown-blanket-hammocks off the face of the cliff, and Fishlegs was so exhausted he fell asleep immediately, as did the Windwalker a little way away, balanced precariously on a tiny ledge, and Toothless, curled up under Hiccup's waistcoat.

Hiccup took a little longer to fall asleep, swinging from the hammock like he was on the deck of his father's ship The Blue Whale.

He looked out over the jagged slit of the gorge laid out beneath him just like it was indeed one of Thor's thunderbolts, and as if he really was a Boy of

Destiny, and the god himself had reached down to earth and was striking Hiccup with his lightning.

And when, finally, he did fall asleep, it was with Old Wrinkly's words going round and round in his head.

'Terrible danger awaits you at the Flashburn School of Swordfighting... The world will need a Hero, and it might as well be you... And remember, look after your sword, Hiccup, for it is the sword that points the way... the sword that points the way... the sword that points the way...'

Tonguetwisters

~ STATISTICS ~

FEAR FACTOR: 9
ATTACK: 9
SPEED: 7
SIZE: 8
DISOBEDIENCE: 9

Tonguetwisters are gigantic
mountain-dwelling dragons. They twist
off their victims' limbs with their long
muscly tongues, thus rendering them
helpless and unable to move.

3. GRAPPLING WITH THE PROBLEM

Now there you are, you see. That
explains what Hiccup was doing
three quarters of the way up Angry
Mountain, and that some sort of
danger awaited him up at the
Flashburn School of Swordfighting.

If, of course, they ever even
made it to the Flashburn School of
Swordfighting.

Now, where were we?

Oh, yes, the revolting Tonguetwister had slid its
tongue around Hiccup's arm as he dangled from the
hammock, completely vulnerable, and suspended over
a three-thousand-foot drop.

The dragon had paused, its disgusting mouth
open with black saliva dripping from its fangs.

All seven of its eyes were focused on Hiccup's
sword, and his sword alone.

The dragon shifted its grip a moment, preparing
to twist off the whole arm with the sword…

And Toothless, who
had given up trying to wake the
Windwalker, realized that he would
have to take drastic action himself.

He leapt up and bit the dragon as hard as
he could right on the tip of that disgusting tongue.
The dragon gave an ear-splitting scream of pain, the
tongue unwrapped itself in a flurry of splattering black
saliva, and the Tonguetwister lost his grip on Hiccup's
arm AND the rock and fell into freefall off the cliff.

'Thanks, Toothless,' breathed Hiccup, and he
gave a final lurching desperate swing, and landed on
the ledge just at the moment that the hammock finally
gave way.

In an instant, the now furious Tonguetwister
pulled out of freefall and was flying back up towards
them with bat-like flaps, murder in its seven eyes.
Hiccup could see the entire swarm had come out of
the Prey Dive and were following.

What were they after?

67

Hiccup thought extremely fast.

'*Look after your sword...*' Old Wrinkly had said. '*For it is the sword that points the way...*'

Suddenly, Hiccup understood. The dragons hadn't been looking at *him*. What they wanted was his *sword*.

'HERE'S MY SWORD IF YOU WANT IT!' yelled Hiccup, leaning backwards, and with one swift sleight of hand, drawing Fishlegs's sword out of his backpack. He held it aloft for a moment to make sure the dragons had seen it and then he threw it as far as he could down into the Gorge.

It made a beautiful arc as it fell.

The multiple dragon eyes snapped like clockwork to the sword.

The lead Tonguetwister leapt after the dropping sword, and the other dragons swarmed after it too, snapping and snarling and pushing one another out of the way, like dogs chasing a stick.

That'll keep them busy for a minute or so before they realize it's the wrong one, thought Hiccup.

'I... can't... hold... on... much... longer...' panted Snotlout, nostrils flaring, eyes popping, teeth gritted. 'Save me, you useless twerp...'

He's far too heavy for me to pull him up, thought Hiccup.

68

As he looked around desperately, he saw beside him on the ledge the ropes and grappling hooks he and Fishlegs had used on the climb. With frantic fingers, Hiccup tied one end to a splinter of rock protruding from the cliff and dangled the grappling hook over the edge of the ledge, as if he were trying to catch a crab at the pier.

'Aaaaaaaaaghghggh!' screamed Snotlout, as his fingers finally gave way. But just at the moment that they did, the grappling hook caught Snotlout's belt, firmly, and held... and he swung out, swinging from the rock by his waist.

OK. So, Snotlout was safe now... for the moment at least.

But the situation could still be described as not good.

Not good at all.

Those dragons were coming back.

Just as soon as they discovered that they were going after the wrong sword, they would be back.

And the Warriors-to-Be were stuck there, unable to move. It would be like shooting fish in a barrel.

'Toothless!' Hiccup ordered. 'I want you to fly as quickly as possible up to the school, find my father, find Flashburn, find ANYONE and make it clear we need rescuing.'

'OK,' squeaked Toothless, unexpectedly obedient, and he zoomed off, deeply relieved to have an excuse to get out of there.

All the young Warriors were awake now, and most had climbed out of their hammocks and taken up as firm a foothold as they could on the cliff, their bows loaded, their spears and swords drawn.

The hunting-dragons too were wide awake, their necks swollen, ready for the next attack, peering down into the darkness of the Gorge.

There were yellow pinpricks in that darkness that grew into eyes.

And a chanting that began softly and grew louder.

'Here they co-o-o-o-o-o-o-o-o-o-ome!' yelled a young Danger-Brute. 'Brace yourselves!'

'MAKE RED your claws
with HUMAN BLOOD...
OBLITERATE the HUMAN FILTH...
Torch the humans like a WOOD
The REBELLION is COMING...'

And a great wave of dragons came roaring up for another attack, pouring out fire before they even reached the cliff.

This time the Vikings' hunting-dragons came flying out to meet them. Smaller though they were, they flew aggressively to meet the onrushing dragons, screaming defiance.

One went down in a blaze of flames, a huge Monstrous Nightmare belonging to Very Vicious the

Visithug, which sank its teeth into the neck of a much larger Grimwing, which then gripped it round the throat, and snapping, biting, screaming, down they went, doomed, into the Gorge in a somersaulting ball of fire.

The attack was fierce and furious but it did not last long. The rebel dragons were beaten back this time, and up they soared, a huge dragon battalion flying in rough formation, up into the sky and then diving down again back into the Gorge.

There was no applause from the panting, embattled young Warriors as the dragons retreated and disappeared, for they knew that this was just a temporary relief, and the dragons would attack again, and again and again, until there was not a human being left on that cliff.

This was how dragons fought.

Hiccup had seen it all his life. A dragon attacked in waves, engaging, and then retreating, and then attacking again, like a cat playing with a mouse.

The ragged line of young Warriors clinging precariously to that cliff-face was a pathetic sight now, heaving for breath, hair singed, faces raked with blood gashes, their hunting-dragons with great livid green

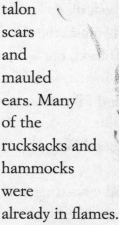

talon
scars
and
mauled
ears. Many
of the
rucksacks and
hammocks
were
already in flames.

The silence
on that cliff-face
spoke volumes. These
young people had been
brought up since babyhood
in a battle society. They were
outnumbered and they knew
they wouldn't be able to hold out
until rescue came. They were done
for. It would take a miracle to save
them now.

Someone started singing, softly,
defiantly, as they hung there in the
tension of the waiting.

'I was born a Hero and a Hero I will die,
Let me join the Heroes who are living in the sky,
You can take away my bright red blood, but a
Hero I remain,
Just let my world be free again, and I'll not have
died in vain...'

'What do we do now then, Snotlout?' Very
Vicious the Visithug called down.

Snotlout had drawn his sword and was struggling
to look dignified, but this is very difficult when you
are hanging by your waistband from a hook, your legs
dangling uselessly, with an arrow poking out of one
of them.

Furthermore, he had just been through a very
trying experience and he hadn't a clue what they should
do next, so for once in his life he was slightly lost for
words. He just opened his mouth and shut it again like
a fish on a hook.

At last he gasped out, 'Ready for battle, men!'
which wasn't very helpful under the circumstances.

'We're not all men, boyo!' shouted down
Camicazi, grinning her battle smile. 'What do
you think, Hiccup?'

Now, you see, Hiccup wasn't as good as Snotlout

in the Looking-Tough-and-Posing-with-your-Skeleton-Tattoos department. But he was considerably better at the Cunning-Plans-Dreamt-Up-in-the-Heat-of-Battle department. Which, some might say, was more useful in a leader.

A leader has to use the equipment he has to hand, and the territory to his advantage.*

Hmmm.
Let's see now.
They outnumber
us four to one,
they have
wings, talons,
teeth and
Fire and we
have... ?

Hiccup's eyes fell on the grappling hooks.

'Listen, everybody!' Hiccup

THIS??

shouted up the cliff. 'Attach your grappling hooks to the ropes that tie you all together! And tie the other end to any rocks or boulders you can find – the bigger the better!'

The young Warriors were desperate now, and in a mood to listen to any plan, however ludicrous or dangerous, so with frantic fingers they did as Hiccup had ordered.

'When the dragons strike,' yelled Hiccup, 'I want you to get in close and throw your grappling hooks on to their backs.'

Down in the Gorge a warning hum, a distant threatening whirr, a glow of yellow appearing in the gloom...

'Here they come aga-a-a-a-a-in!' yelled the Danger-Brute, and the Warriors swallowed, put back their shoulders, and tried to get a firm foothold on the cliff and a close grip on their grappling hooks.

Up the mighty battalion of dragons flew, closer still and closer.

'Wait... wait... wait...' shouted Hiccup.

Then when the dragons were almost upon them, 'Throw your hooks!'

All along the cliff the Warriors threw the

grappling hooks with the long ropes, up on to the attacking dragons, as if they were living dragon mountains, or moving fiery buildings.

Some of the grappling hooks missed their moving targets, or slid harmlessly, bouncing off the dragons' backs. But many more hit home, lodging on to one of the spiny back fins as if it were a ledge, or burying their sharp pointed edges into the tough dragon flesh of a leg or a shoulder.

As before, the leader dragon trumpeted 'Retreat!' and the dragons disengaged to soar upwards as they had previously, intending to dive back into the Gorge and mount yet another attack.

But that was not quite what happened.

Up the dreadful dragon battalion rose, blazing triumphantly with fire, chanting or screaming with victory, leaving the burning wreckage of their victims on the cliff as they prepared to re-mount the attack...

But many of the dragons were caught by the grappling hooks and with them the ropes, and at the other ends, the boulders. As the dragons rose, so the ropes first tightened, then, one by one, snapped the stones from the ledges.

All at once, the air was a tapestry of

criss-crossing bonds and boulders catapulting across the sky. The dragons shrieked in alarm as the boulders smashed against one, then another, and the ropes whiplashed against heads and wings and talons.

The frightened dragons fought to pull away, and when they could not, they turned and attacked one another, or entangled other dragons in the mess of ropes.

The dragon leader, realizing what had happened, screeched for the dragons to stay calm, to pull together, not to panic. But the dragons had not flown together long enough for that. And if dragons hate anything, it is being bound or chained. The ropes terrified them, and pandemonium broke out.

One moment they were a victorious, soaring, dragon battalion. The next, to the joyous amazement of the young Heroes on the rock-face, they were a chaos of shrieking dragons fighting tooth and talon to get free, and dragon after dragon breaking out of the ropes and deserting, streaking for the horizon... The Sagas may tell a different story. But *that* was how Hiccup the Third won the Battle of Angry Mountain, leading a troop of youngsters clinging to a cliff, against a dragon foe that outnumbered them four to one.

Using only some old grappling
hooks and ropes.

The
Second
to the
Left
Tower

Witch's
Fortune
Telling Hut

Flashburn's School

The
Battle
Arena

Banqueting
Hall

of Swordfighting

4. A GAME OF HIDE-AND-SEEK

Just as the Rogue dragons disappeared, and the cliff-face rang out with the young Warriors' cheers, the Windwalker *finally* woke up.

'Oh, have I missed something?' he asked innocently.

Snotlout was still dangling from the tree below Hiccup, and he had to be rescued by Very Vicious and Thuggory and a couple more of the bulkiest Meatheads and Visithugs who climbed down to help pull him up.

For some reason they seemed to think that it was quite funny that Snotlout was suspended from the cliff by his underpants with an arrow sticking out of his calf.

'HA HA HA HA HA HA HA!' Very Vicious and Thuggory roared with laughter. 'You look just like a fishy on a hook!'

'You will regret this, cousin of mine,' Snotlout promised himself, removing the arrow from his leg. 'Just you wait. You will regret this, Hiccup, and my time will come.'

But in his wounded state, he allowed himself to

be flown up to the top of the cliff on the back of the Windwalker nonetheless.

It was only one o'clock in the morning, but nobody felt like hanging around in case those Rogue dragons came back, and besides, most of the hammocks had been burnt to ashes. So the young Warriors climbed the rest of the cliff in the darkness of the night-time, and it was quite tricky, for they had so few of the grappling hooks and ropes left.

They reached the Flashburn School of Swordfighting by about six o'clock, according to Hiccup's ticking-thing, and by then the young Warriors were a pathetic, bedraggled sight.

It was the largest castle that Hiccup had ever seen. It was also strangely silent.

They cried up at the walls to be let in, for the drawbridge to be let down, but the great grey walls answered them not. Up on the battlements, flocks of Neverbirds nesting in the towers above and awoken by the commotion, called back with their own longing, melancholy cries, which sound remarkably like: 'Where are yo-o-o-o-ou??'

The exhausted young Warriors threw up their grappling hooks, scaled the castle walls, and collapsed, exhausted, on the battlements.

'I thought we'd really had it that time,' gasped
Fishlegs.

Fishlegs was sprawled beside Hiccup.

He had lost his helmet, and his dragon
Horrorcow had been so frightened
when she heard the words
of the Rogue dragons
at the cliff-face that
she had flown on
top of Fishlegs's
head and entwined
her claws into
his hair for safety,
mooing in a terrified
way. (Infant dragons
often climb on to their
mother's back or head
and cling to it in times of
peril.)

Camicazi was so beside
herself with over-excitement,
she was chattering even
quicker than normal.

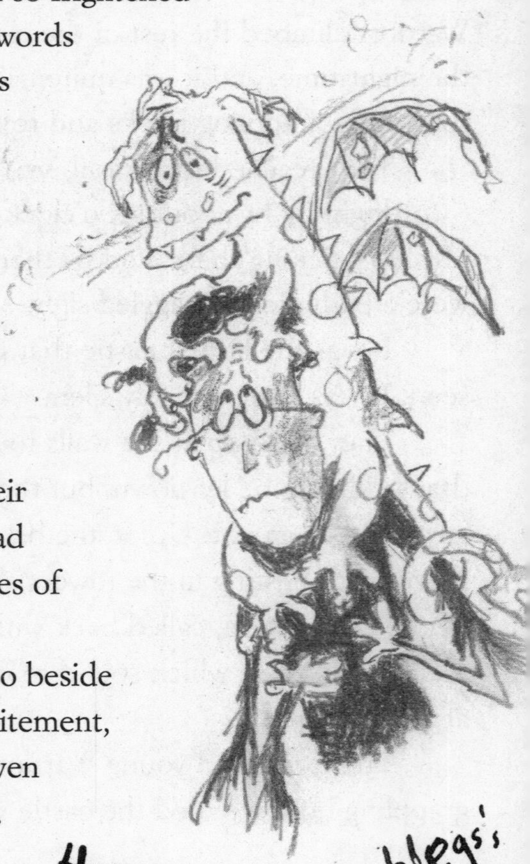

Horrorcow attached to Fishlegs's head

'You were brilliant, Hiccup, brilliant! That whole grappling-hook thing was awesome!'

Even in his ragged, singed, exhausted state, Hiccup felt triumphant.

Now that they were safe, the young Warriors came over to thump Hiccup on the back and thank him for his idea about the grappling hooks.

'Um… good work, what's-your-name, Hiccup?' grunted Very Vicious the Visithug gruffly, slapping him on the back so hard he nearly fell over. 'Sorry about the misunderstanding earlier…'

'I told you,' grinned Thuggory the Meathead. 'He's surprisingly cool.'

Hiccup wasn't used to getting this kind of attention from the tougher, older Vikings. Normally, at best, they ignored him, or at worst, laughed and jeered.

This was what my father meant about getting the respect of my peer-group, thought Hiccup, red with embarrassment and pride.

It felt good.

But he still had a feeling of terrible unease at the edges of his mind. He had defeated those dragons… *for now…* but why were different species flying side by side to attack the Warriors in the first place? Why did they want Hiccup's sword? And what was that horrible thing that they were chanting in Dragonese?

And it wasn't long before the Warriors stopped congratulating each other, and started looking around at their surroundings questioningly. What was going on? Where was everybody?

Camicazi's excited chattering died away.

The silence was deathly.

They had never been to the Flashburn School before, but they knew there ought to have been look-outs on the battlements, even at night-time. Where were they? There were spears neatly stacked, and shields balanced as if someone had just put them away tidily.

But nobody was there.

And Old Wrinkly had said that terrible danger awaited them at the Flashburn School of Swordfighting... thought Hiccup.

A flap of wings, and Hiccup jumped...

But it was only Toothless, coming to sit on Hiccup's helmet, looking very relaxed and pleased with himself, and eating what looked like an enormous mouthful of wild boar.

'Where have you been?' asked Hiccup, a little irritated. 'I asked you to get *help*, not get yourself some breakfast, we were in real trouble down there!'

Toothless started guiltily. 'Oh yes, Toothless was looking. Toothless l-l-looked EVERYWHERE.'

'Why is your mouth full?' asked Hiccup sternly.

'Not eating,' explained Toothless, batting his eyelids innocently. 'Just ch-ch-chewing the air.'

'Well that air smells like wild boar,' said Hiccup.

"N-n-not eating," said Toothless, batting his eyelids innocently.

87

Surely a dragoN
this cute could never
tell a LiE ??

'HELLLLOOOOOO!' shouted Thuggory the Meathead. 'IS THERE ANYBODY HE-E-E-ERE? COME OUT AND DECLARE YOURSELVES!'

Answer came there none.

'Whe-e-e-ere *a-a-a-a-are* yo-o-o-o-ouuuu?' called the Neverbirds.

The young Warriors looked at one another.

Perhaps they weren't safe after all.

Nobody said it, but what they were thinking was: *Maybe there are some of those Rogue dragons even here, in this very castle...*

They drew their swords, and began to wander cautiously through the deserted building.

But everywhere they went all they met was silence, apart from the howling of the wind, and the cry of the Neverbirds:

'Where a-a-a-are yo-o-o-o-o-o-ouuuu?'

Which was unfortunately rather appropriate for the slightly sinister game of hide-and-seek they were playing, and didn't help their nerves.

It is a spooky experience, tip-toeing through the darkness of an unfamiliar abandoned castle in the dead of night, not knowing whether someone or something may jump out at you at any moment.

The young Warriors were experienced burglars and soldiers, of course, so they crept through the castle like seasoned commandos. Two of them stood on either side of a door, and then they all burst through, axes and swords at the ready, and checked under tables, behind doors, beneath tapestries. Nothing.

'Where a-a-a-are y-o-o-o-o-o-o-ouuu?' croaked the Neverbirds.

Hiccup's back was tense, nerves as tight as catgut, expecting at any moment dragon claws upon his back, dragon fire upon his neck.

There were great training rooms with swords and spears stacked in racks on the side, huge empty towers, and an enormous central fighting arena with torches flaming all around it. Someone must have lit those torches. But where were all the people?

Finally, having wandered for half an hour through echoing halls and the warren of empty corridors, Hiccup's and Very Vicious's Warriors-to-Be all met somewhere in the middle, outside a great glowing-windowed banqueting hall.

Just as Hiccup's nerves could barely stand it, there was a whirr of wings overhead, somebody cried out 'DRAGONS!' and a number of tense young Warriors-to-Be let fly their Northbows without thinking.

'WODEN'S WHISKERS, DON'T FIRE, YOU IMBECILES, YOU NEARLY TOOK MY HEAD OFF THERE!' yelled a furious voice from above. It was Stoick the Vast, aboard his great dragon Bullheart. 'OPEN THE CASTLE DOORS!'

The adult Warriors, who had taken the Easy Way up Angry Mountain, were arriving. As they staggered through the castle doors it was clear that the Easy Way had not been all that easy, what with one thing and another.

The adults had been attacked by Rogue dragons, too.

Scorched faces, riding-dragons that limped with scarred limbs and red-ripped ears, someone rather inexplicably carrying a blackened, burnt piece of mast still with the flag flying bravely from the end, shell-shocked, serious... this was the state in which the adult Warriors arrived.

The tired Chieftains' expressions were unusually grim as they landed their riding-dragons on the battle arena. Wordlessly, they took in the state of their young Warriors-to-Be, ash-streaked and bleeding, raked with talons and blasted by fire, their clothes flapping in rags about them, still coughing from the smoke – all unmistakeable signs of a full-scale dragon attack.

The Warriors-to-Be were tough young adolescents, but even though they were trying to carry their broken weapons with their usual swagger, their eyes betrayed them. You could see the fear in those eyes from their extraordinarily close brush with death.

They were scared.

Dragons had never behaved in this way before. An attack of this nature, with different species joining together, was unheard of in the Archipelago.

And they were terrified it was going to happen again...

'Are you all alive?' growled Bertha, Chief of the Bog-Burglars and Camicazi's mother, a great thunder-thighed mountain of a woman, whose singed plaits were still smoking slightly.

Camicazi stepped forward, and gave the salute. 'All alive,' she said, 'thanks to Hiccup Horrendous Haddock the Third. But the castle is deserted.'

That really rattled the Chieftains.

'Biceps of Thor!' bellowed Mogadon the Meathead. 'Don't tell me Flashburn has been defeated!

Impossible! The finest Hero the Archipelago has ever known! And his forty Warriors, and the Red Tigers... They're undefeatable. How can this be?'

Together, they pushed wide the gigantic door of the banqueting hall, as tall as a house.

C-r-e-a-a-a-a-k...

Nobody there again.

There was a big golden cauldron sitting on the remains of an extinguished fire, but the ashes were still smouldering.

The long table was set for a great triumphal banquet, the Banquet of the New Warriors – and a joyous feast it should have been indeed, with the torches lit, and a thousand Vikings toasting the new generation.

The Tribes of the Archipelago trooped into that banqueting hall in funereal procession and surveyed what ought to have been the triumphal feast.

The food was set on the long tables. A great wild boar sitting in the middle – with a few little gummy bites taken out of it, but that would have been Toothless. Nobber Nobrains found a chicken leg and gnawed on it enthusiastically.

'Mmmm... tasty... and still warm,' he grunted.

93

Still warm… that meant the inhabitants of the castle had been there very recently.

But where were they now?

'Where a-a-a-are yo-o-o-o-o-o-ouu?' the distant song of the Neverbirds floated hauntingly through the window.

It was a mystery.

KNOCK! KNOCK! KNOCK!

The noise came out of nowhere, an imperious, ringing knock, like the great god Thor knocking on a metal door with the tip of his axe.

Sounding out in a deserted castle on a cliff-top with the wind howling around them and the inhabitants of that castle having mysteriously disappeared, the effect on the exhausted Vikings who had spent the night fighting Rogue dragons, well, the effect on those Vikings was pretty devastating, I'd say.

KNOCK! KNOCK! KNOCK!

'What was that?' whispered Grabbit the
Grim, his two black-and-blue eyes boggling, his grip
tightening on his still-smouldering axe. 'What was that
noise?'

KNOCK! KNOCK! KNOCK!

'There it is again!' exclaimed Stoick in
astonishment.

It was a loud, echoing noise, as if someone was
knocking on a metal door, and expecting an answer.

KNOCK! KNOCK! KNOCK!

'Where *a-a-a-re* y-o-o-o-o-o-uuuuu...........?'
'Where could it possibly be coming from?'
wondered Stoick.

Uh oh, thought Hiccup.

'Maybe its Fishlegs's knees knocking together,'
suggested Snotlout, but he said it with less than usual
swagger in his sneer because there was something
deeply unsettling and spooky about such a knocking in
such a setting.

95

KNOCK! KNOCK! KNOCK!

'Well, shiver my cockles and blister my bunions, it seems to be coming from the cauldron!' exclaimed Stoick.

KNOCK! KNOCK! KNOCK!

It was indeed coming from the big golden cauldron.

Something or someone was inside that cauldron, and that something or someone was knocking the insides, with a clear, loud knock.

'Investigate the cauldron, Nobrains!' ordered Stoick.

'Um... I've got a little cramp in my leg actually, Chief,' said Nobber. 'Old war injury... it comes on occasionally...'

The Vikings had been brought up on stories by the fireside of skeletons being brought back to life in a cooking pot, so they could hardly be blamed for their terror.

The Chiefs looked at one another. They stepped forward to the cauldron.

The golden cauldron was surrounded by eighteen muscled Chieftains with their weapons drawn, not to mention most of the Warriors in the Archipelago.

Grabbit the Grim threw back his shoulders and knocked on the lid himself, three bright bossy knocks.

He cleared his throat importantly.

'Come out, whoever you are!' he ordered. 'This is Chief Grabbit the Grim speaking! Come out with your hands above your head, for you are surrounded!'

The cauldron was abruptly silent.

This time Stoick knocked.

'If you don't come out on the count of three,' he warned, in his most important I-Must-Be-Obeyed voice, 'we will be forced to lift the lid ourselves, and I warn you, we are very heavily armed...'

Silence from the cauldron.

Well, those eighteen hairy Chieftains would rather have been blown by storms into the back of next week before they lost face in front of one another. They were a-feared, oh yes they were. They were a-feared right down to their unkempt toenails,

97

but they were going to lift that lid anyway, even if there were one hundred ghosts inside, having degenerate ghost parties with their ancestors.

'Mogadon! Murderous!' said Stoick imperiously. 'Help me lift the lid…'

'Oh, don't lift the lid… *Please* don't lift the lid…' Poor Fishlegs was practically crying he was so frightened, and Hiccup had to agree with him. It seemed a good idea to keep that cauldron shut.

Don't open the cauldron… don't open the cauldron…

The lid was so heavy it took all three Vikings to he-e-e-eave it off the cauldron, and it clanged to the deck with a great ringing clamour…

… and the three Vikings bellowed as if they were one Viking…

… as something flew out of the cauldron…

'A chicken!' yelled Baggybum in relief. 'It's only a chicken!'

'Only a chicken! HA! HA! HA! HA! HA!' boomed the Vikings, hugely embarrassed and relieved. 'HA! HA! HA! HA! HA!'

When…

'Hang on a second,' squeaked Fishlegs in alarm, 'there's something else in there!'

And there it was, clawing out of the cauldron and grasping hold of the rim from the inside with a ghastly, groping grasp.

A human hand, with fingernails tipped with iron.

5. SOMETHING NASTY IN THE CAULDRON

'AAAAAAARGGGGHHHHHH!' screamed the
Hooligans, the Murderous and the Grims, the
Bog-Burglars, the Silents, the Bashem-Oiks, and the
other Tribes of the Archipelago, stampeding around
the banqueting hall like panicking water buffalos as
the white hand stretched towards them.

'Ghosts and ghouls...' breathed Stoick the Vast
through white lips, '... born out of the cooking pot...'

Snaggletooth jumped right into Gobber's arms,
and appeared to be trying to climb on top of his head.

Baggybum the Beerbelly attempted to climb
under a bench, and jammed there, tight as a cork in a
bottle.

In fascinated horror, Hiccup fixed his eyes on a
second outstretched hand, white as coral, and covered
with an unidentified grey-green slime of some sort,
as it shakily re-e-e-eached out of the cauldron and
grasped the edge of the rim.

And slowly, slowly, up out of the cooking pot,
there rose a human head as paper white and grinning

There was
something
NASTY
in
thE
Cauldron

as a skull. And as the figure rose higher and higher, they saw it was the figure of an old woman, with long white hair, and half-blind eyes covered with a thick grey layer of scum, and a nose as sharp as the point of a knife.

'A ghost! A ghost! A ghost!' screamed the Vikings.

For the old woman was skinny as a skeleton, and her grey breast-plate and long white robes and malevolent expression were exactly the sort of things you might expect a ghost to be wearing.

Hiccup was peering through his fingers now, and he let out a gasp as he suddenly realized that this wasn't a ghost at all. In fact, it was something considerably worse than a ghost. It made an undead warrior ghost from Valhalla look like a fluffy little kitten on a play-date.

Still so painfully white, so drained of colour that Hiccup could hardly bear to look at her. The bones so close under the skin that it was like staring straight at a skull, tapping fingernails tipped with iron.

'Dear oh dear oh dear oh dear oh dear!' exclaimed Hiccup in horror and surprise. '*It's Alvin the Treacherous's mother!*'

Well might Hiccup be horrified and surprised.

For Alvin the Treacherous's mother was a thoroughly unpleasant and powerful witch, and Hiccup had thought that she was dead.

If *she* was alive, that meant that her son Alvin was too, and this was VERY BAD NEWS INDEED, for Alvin the Treacherous was Hiccup's arch-enemy...

'Do you know this ghost, Hiccup?' asked Stoick the Vast in amazement.

'It's not a ghost at all,' said Hiccup. 'It's Alvin the Treacherous's mother, and she's a very dangerous witch.'

'It's not a ghost, guys! It's only a witch!' yelled out Mogadon the Meathead in relief.

The dripping witch slithered her way out of the cauldron.

In front of their astonished eyes she scuttled across the hall on all fours like a dog or a wolf, her iron fingernails clicking on the stone floor. Oh, it sent a shiver down the spine, to see the way she moved, like a beetle or an evil thing, not like a human at all.

She sat on the chair at the head of the table. She tipped her head to one side, waiting for questions.

She got them.

'Madam!' bellowed Stoick the Vast, with a strong sense of injury. 'You owe us an explanation! What on earth are you doing popping out of cauldrons and frightening us at this late hour?'

The witch's voice sent chills down the spine, something between a hiss and a whisper, with just that edge of evil to it that makes you sit up straight and check that your soul is still intact, and that she hasn't sucked it out of you while you weren't watching.

'My name is Excellinor, and I am the castle's witch. I do not like,' said the witch, her voice as dry as ice, 'either to pop into or to pop out of cauldrons. However, the castle was invaded by dragons of the most dreadful and dangerous kind. Flashburn and his Warriors were defeated and there were no survivors, apart from myself, for I had the foresight to creep inside this cooking pot, and hide myself just in time…'

Hiccup looked around the room. No flame marks, no over-turned chairs, no blood, no sign of a struggle of any sort.

She lied.

But why would the Vikings not believe her? They had just had the most terrible and bloody battle against Rogue dragons themselves. What was more natural than that Flashburn and his Warriors had been carried off by those very same dragons?

Uproar in the banqueting hall. Cries of: 'Carried off, by my trousers!' and 'We must avenge!'

'But why?' asked a bewildered Grim-bod. 'Why is this happening? What is going on?'

The witch's half-blind eyes gleamed.

'Someone has set free the Dragon Furious from the prison of Berserk, and he is bringing a Dragon Rebellion that will kill us all...' hissed the witch.

Gasps of horror from the Viking Tribes.

Oh dear, oh dear, OH DEAR... *So that* WAS *the Dragon Furious who attacked us on the cliff*, thought Hiccup.

'What you have seen in those dragons is the coming of the Red-Rage,' said the witch.

'And what,' asked Stoick the Vast, not really wanting to know the answer to this question, 'what exactly is the Red-Rage?'

'The Red-Rage is where the dragons mass together in a pack to hunt down their prey. No quarter is given,' smiled the witch Excellinor. 'The only aim is to hunt down every man, woman and child until they become extinct.'

Silence in the banqueting hall as the Tribes tried to take this in.

'DO-O-O-O-OM!!'

screamed the witch, her voice the spine-jingling scratch of nails on a blackboard. 'DOOOM HAS COME TO THE ARCHIPELAGO!'

'Nonsense,' blustered Stoick. 'The dragons are just getting a bit frisky, that's all…'

'Ask your son,' whispered the witch. 'For he it was who set the dragon free…' she said joyfully.

Oh, brother.

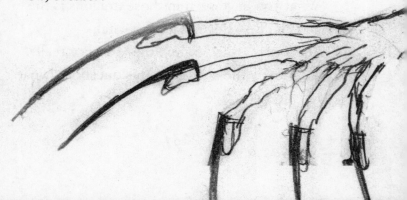

The
Witch
Excellinor

There was a collective gasp of horror and to Hiccup's utter, cringing, burning embarrassment all the Tribes of the Archipelago turned round to stare down at him, tutting furiously and pointing their fingers and shaking their heads.

That was all it took. Only a couple of hours earlier Hiccup had been the Hero who had saved all the young Warriors at the Battle of Angry Mountain.

Now, in an instant, that was all forgotten and he was the idiot who had put them all in deadly peril by setting free the Dragon Furious.

Hiccup turned absolutely flame red, right to the tips of his ears, and wished he could disappear up the chimney.

'*He* spoke to the Dragon Furious,' hissed the witch. 'Ask Hiccup Horrendous Haddock the Third what the dragon said to him about the Rebellion.'

'What did the dragon say, Hiccup?' Stoick turned to his son.

'Well, I've been trying to tell you that for ages, Father,' Hiccup burst out, squirming uncomfortably. 'The dragon said that we had one year before he returned to wipe out the whole of the human race. But that was such a long time ago, and the year passed, and I sort of hoped that maybe he'd forgotten about it...'

Another terrible silence. Stoick the Vast made a noise like an exploding kettle.

Most fathers would agree with his frustration.

THE dESTRUCTION OF THE ENTIRE HUMAN RACE ???? YOU'D HAVE THOUGHT THAT WAS IMPORTANT ENOUGH TO MENTION IN PASSING!!

'HOW COULD YOU POSSIBLY KEEP SOMETHING LIKE THIS FROM ME? THE EXTINCTION OF THE ENTIRE HUMAN RACE! YOU'D HAVE THOUGHT THAT WAS IMPORTANT ENOUGH TO MENTION IN PASSING!'

'I did mention it, but you were always too busy to listen,' Hiccup pointed out miserably.

Stoick controlled himself with a strong effort.

'What should we do, O Great Prophetess?' asked Mogadon the Meathead, speaking for all of the Tribes. 'How can we prevent this terrible thing from happening?'

The witch smiled, and *what* a nasty smile it was.

'You need a new King of the Wilderwest.'

Uproar in the banqueting hall.

Cries of 'Never! Never again shall we have a King!'

The Tribes of the Archipelago were an independent lot, who spent their whole time burgling and fighting each other. They did not want a King to boss them around and tell them what to do. They hadn't had a King of the Wilderwest for many years and they didn't want to start having one now.

In fact, this kind of talk had got the witch into terrible trouble in the past. UG the Uglithug, the King of the Mainland, had only had to hear her talk of Prophecies and a new King, and he had imprisoned her in a tree trunk for twenty years.

But timing is everything. *Now* all the witch had to do was stick her finger in the air and hiss:

'DOOMED! WE ARE ALL DOOMED IF WE DO NOT DO THIS!'

And because of their recent mauling at the hands of the Red-Rage dragons, everyone fell magically silent.

'Only the King can save us now. And luckily,' purred the witch, 'the LAST King of the Wilderwest, Grimbeard the Ghastly, left behind a certain Prophecy. A Prophecy that has been handed down from witch to witch for generation after generation...'

'Tell us the Prophecy, O Great Sorceress!' cried the Vikings.

The witch leant forward, and she whispered these words, as if she were telling them a wonderful secret, and in the quietness of that banqueting hall the Vikings leant in to hear the witch speak as the fire crackled and the wind howled.

'The Dragontime is coming
And only a King can save you now.
The King shall be the
Champion of Champions.

You shall know the King
By the King's Lost Things.
A fang-free dragon, my second-best sword,
My Roman shield,
An arrow-from-the-land-that-does-not-exist,
The heart's stone, the key-that-opens-all-locks,
The ticking-thing, the Throne, the Crown.

And last and best of all the ten,
The Dragon Jewel shall save all men.'

Hiccup was finding it difficult to stand up
straight. He felt a bit like some invisible net had risen
up around him and was trying to choke him.

The witch was a spider, spinning her story-web
through the room, weaving it in and out of the
Vikings' ears like smoke. And he was part of that story,

114

a story that he felt up until then, like his boat *The Hopeful Puffin*, had been turning round in random circles, but in fact might have a purpose, a pattern that he had not previously seen or understood.

For *Hiccup* had Grimbeard's second-best sword hidden in his scabbard, Grimbeard's smashed ticking-thing tucked into his waistcoat, a rectangular Roman shield with a dent squashed in it by Dogsbreath the Duhbrain in his right hand, an arrow from America, the land-that-does-not-exist, sitting in his quiver, the key-that-opens-all-locks hanging from his belt, half a ruby heart's stone in the bracelet round his arm, a toothless dragon flying above him...

The King's Lost Things.

Impossible... thought Hiccup. *Impossible... I found all of these things by accident! I wasn't even looking for them...* *

'There are no accidents,' said the witch grimly, as if Hiccup had spoken aloud.

What is she up to? thought Hiccup, standing as still as a statue turned to stone by a gorgon. *Why does she want me to be the King? Is that really Grimbeard's Prophecy, or has she just made that all up? And if she already knows what the right things are, why doesn't*

---

* If you read Hiccup's eight previous adventures, listed at the front of this book, you can find out where and how Hiccup found these Things.

she just steal them off me?

Nobody was thinking of Hiccup, apart from Fishlegs and Camicazi, who were staring at him with their mouths wide open. Hiccup shook his head at them to tell them not to say anything.

Everybody else was far too busy thinking what a great King of the Wilderwest they themselves would make to notice that there was one among them who already had most of the King's Lost Things.

And why would they think that Hiccup's smashed-up, bashed-up possessions were equipment fit for a King? Of course they wouldn't.

And how could they imagine that the new King of the Wilderwest would be a skinny little thirteen-year-old whose fault this all was in the first place? Again, of course they couldn't, it was the last thing on their minds.

'But this is impossible!' cried a Grim-bod. 'Arrows from a land that does not exist? Keys that open all locks? Heart's stones? Ticking-things? Fairy tales and fiddle-sticks! How are we to get hold of all of these things in time before this Red-Rage builds and this Furious Dragon attacks, with even more power next time? And what can this King do to stop him anyway?'

The King's Lost Things

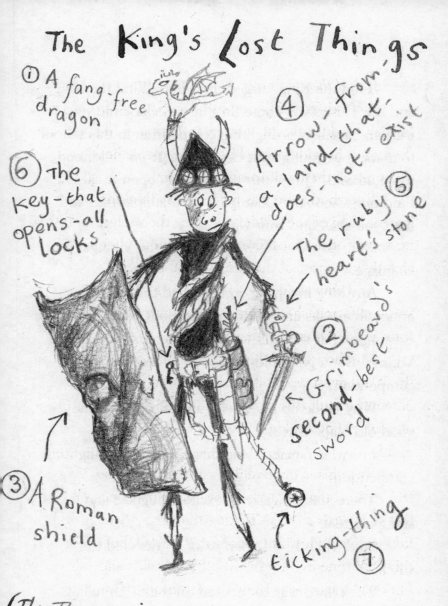

① A fang-free dragon

⑥ the key-that opens-all locks

④ Arrow, from a-land-that-does-not-exist

⑤ The ruby heart's stone

② ← Grimbeard's second-best sword

③ A Roman shield

← Eicking-thing ⑦

(The Throne is safe in Hooligan Harbour. The Crown is hidden below Flashburn School. NOBODY KNOWS where the Dragon Jewel is.)

'Find the King,' urged the witch. 'Find the King, and the Things will come. In three weeks' time you were to have a swordfighting competition in this school to mark your young Warriors moving from childhood to adulthood. Throw this competition open to all... Find out who is the Champion of Champions... and then you shall find your King.'

Well, now the witch was talking the Vikings' language.

Anything involving cunning and brain-power, impossible tasks and riddling talk about lands not existing... that was a little baffling to most of the Vikings. But a good old-fashioned sword-fighting competition?

Why, shine up my shield, and sharpen up the good old blade there!

Everyone fancied their chances in a swordfighting competition.

There was a babble of excited laughter and stamping feet.

'And when I said open to *all*...' drawled the witch.

The crowd was so focused on the witch telling her story, that they had not noticed people creeping in at the door, dropping down from the windows, leaking into the room like rats. People with slit noses, and not enough ears, and teeth that had been filed into points. Some that barked like dogs, or crept on all fours like their mistress.

'*Outcasts…*' breathed Stoick the Vast, and every Viking in the room had drawn their sword already, as you do when you smell a rat.

'But we have turned our backs on these people,' Mogadon the Meathead reminded Excellinor, in his sternest voice. 'They are too villainous, too mean and vicious even for us Vikings.'

'Then maybe you have turned your backs on yourselves!' hissed the witch. 'Perhaps this calamity has come upon you because you have grown soft, and forgotten what it means to be a Viking. Who knows? The gods will tell us, by guiding who wins the competition.'

'Eldest Elder!' boomed Bertha of the Bog-Burglars, addressing the oldest of the Vikings, a tiny, unbelievably wrinkled old Bashem-Oik. 'Surely the Outcasts cannot join in this competition? They are common criminals!'

'Watch your tongue, little Bertha!' swiftly hissed the witch. 'These are my chosen people, and my son Alvin, whom they now recognize' (a particularly nasty note came into her voice, and a few of the Outcasts whimpered) 'once again as their Chief, is a direct descendant of Grimbeard the Ghastly, by his eldest son Thugheart the Treacherous...'

The Eldest Elder sighed.

He had had a hard night fighting Rogue dragons and he was getting way too old for that sort of nonsense.

'I am afraid that this is true. The Outcasts are just as likely to be Heirs as anyone else.'

So that was the witch's game... she wanted her son Alvin to be the King...

Hiccup stole a look at a tall figure who had crept in with the other Outcasts, a figure so shrouded in furs that you could not see who it was – but Hiccup knew.

A protruding tip of a golden nose, the glimpse of an ivory leg, a sliver of a blade beneath the thick black fur, all of that told the story.

Alvin the Treacherous, as I live and breathe...

shrouded all in furs

Slowly Alvin pulled
down his hood to reveal his
wicked face. Bald as an egg,
a smiling villain with too
many teeth, he didn't
seem to have lost
anything this time.
(Alvin had been a
little careless with
his limbs over the years.)
Instead,
he had gained
a rather handsome
wart, right in the
middle of his chin,
caught from
his mother,
perhaps, for
she was covered
with the things.
    'Good
morning, Hiccup

121

Horrendous Haddock the Third,' purred Alvin the Treacherous pleasantly, with a graceful wave of his hook. 'What a very great pleasure to see you again...'

UP the witch jumped on to the banqueting table, kicking aside the cups.

'And now for a pledge, my pretties!' she crowed. 'A pledge by my once-brown eyes! It's not that I don't *trust* you, of course, but we *are* Vikings, after all. Your Chieftains must pledge, on behalf of their Tribes, that whoever wins the swordfight and becomes Champion of Champions, will be the right True King of the Wilderwest, and they will bow down to them as their King.'

The witch's voice was dark now. It would be a hard promise to make, for island Tribesmen were proud of their freedom.

'It must be blood on the paper for this one, none of your spit-and-cross-fingers-nonsense.'

There was paper and ink on the table, which was surprising, because it was a banqueting hall, after all, and the witch made the Eldest Elder write out the pledge right then and there.

Goodness gracious!
It's ALVIN the TREACHEROUS!

The Chieftains looked at each other in the candlelight.

Don't do it! screamed Hiccup's thoughts. But what could he say? He was in a slightly awkward position, because it was him who had set free the Dragon Furious in the first place.

One by one they took the pledge, a swift cut of their swords on their fingers, and the pledge was signed.

Alvin the Treacherous was

Alvin's wooden nose caught fire in the blaze on Berserk so now he has a nose made of GOLD

Hiccup's arch-enemy.
ALVIN the TREACHEROUS.

I PLEDGE that

Whomsoever shall WIN the

Swordfighting Competition on

the New Year's Day shall be

right True King of the Wilderwest

and I shall bow down to them as

my King.

BER THA   Signed: MADguts   STONK
                      the MurdeRUSS   the Vast

Mogadon   DANGEROUS   VIIII   Alvin the Treacherous
           of the Danger   Excellinor the Witch
                      BRUTES
        Underhand the Uglything
           (Stand-In Chief)   Grabbit of Grim

Baily   DeadlyDog   Dillard   Percival Peaceable
of Bashem Chief of Grim   Gentle Quit-Life
           Kyrgzrrengrgthrcrm
              the Yowharm

REMEMBER: A Promise IS a PROMISE,

IF IT IS MaDE In BLOOD.

Not Present: Berserks,
Hysterics, Lava-Louts

the last to sign. He stepped forward with his sword, the Stormblade. The witch took the blade, cut both herself and Alvin's fingers, and pressed both their hands together to the paper.

Oh that was a solemn pledge indeed, a pledge made by eighteen Chieftains on the top of a mountain in the dead of a winter's morning, with the wind howling all around.

You can't break a pledge like that.

And when the Chieftains had made it they gave the paper to the Eldest Elder.

'It's a shame that poor Flashburn can't be here,' sighed Bertha sentimentally. 'He'd win the swordfighting competition and be the Champion of Champions so easily,'

'Yes, *isn't* it a shame he isn't here,' smiled the witch.

'And now... if nobody minds I think I'll head off to bed. Flashburn gave me a small hut just behind the Battle Arena. If anyone wants their fortune read over the next couple of days, or some nutritional advice for the swordfighting competition, well, that's where I'll be...'

And down she dropped on all fours, and scuttled

out of the room, her long white hair dragging in the dust behind her.

An uncomfortable silence descended as she went (no one wanted to mention the on-all-fours thing, but it was a little eccentric, let's face it), and all heaved a sigh of relief as she left, as if something nasty had just left the room.

As indeed it had.

'What are we waiting for?' roared Mogadon the Meathead. 'This IS a funeral after all! LET'S GET FEASTING, EVERYONE!'

So that was how the Banquet of the New Warriors turned into Flashburn's funeral. No one knows how to celebrate a funeral like the Vikings of the Archipelago. Even after being up all night having their horns blown off by rampaging dragons, those Vikings were still up for a party. In fact the tension had given them an appetite. They set about demolishing that banquet, and singing wild sea songs, and dancing

on their battle-sore
feet without a care in
the world.

Hiccup watched them
from by the fire, head in his
hands, his mind racing about
what all this meant. Why did
he have these King's Things?
What was the witch's game?
And when would the Dragon
Furious attack again?

The Outcasts watched the Vikings too, prowling
in the shadows. Alvin was by the door again, in his
furs, tap tap tapping with that ivory leg.

And watchful, ears down, slinking under the
tables, flying at the windows, the hunting-dragons and
the riding-dragons of the Tribes of the Archipelago
watched the merriment as well.

What side would they be on, when the Dragon
Furious attacked? Would they stay faithful to their
Masters, or join in the Rebellion?

Only time would tell.

6. TROUBLE AT THE SCHOOL

'HA! HA! HA! HA! HA! HA!'

It was two weeks after their disastrous arrival at the Flashburn School of Swordfighting. There had been no sign of Rogue dragons chanting the Red-Rage, or the Dragon Furious.

The Warriors-to-Be, from Tribes all across the Archipelago, had gathered in the Battle Arena to watch Fishlegs's practice bout against Lardtummy Lo-Watt. The laughing young Warriors-to-Be were surrounding the fight, and they appeared to be finding it amusing. Watching Fishlegs fight was always the highlight of their day.

Lardtummy Lo-Watt was not a good swordfighter. He was as round as he was high, and so stupid he had been known to attack his own arm.

But Fishlegs had a severe disadvantage.

Horrorcow was still sitting on top of Fishlegs's shoulders, her talons gripped into his hair.

Her nervous collapse was such that even now that the danger had passed, she still refused to eat, sleep or come down, despite Hiccup tempting her with bits of cucumber and carrot. She just sat on

Fishlegs's head, sad and blinking, poor Horrorcow, her tail hanging limply.

'I'm so sorry,' she mooed apologetically, when Hiccup begged her to let go. 'I just can't.'

And if there was a loud noise she clenched her claws, winding Fishlegs's hair around so painfully that he screamed like a hyena.

As you can imagine, none of this improved Fishlegs's swordfighting.

Take it from me, it is extremely difficult to swordfight effectively when you have a dragon attached to your head.

It throws off your balance.

Although opponents did find Fishlegs's sudden inexplicable girly screaming off-putting.

Plus Hiccup had thrown Fishlegs's best sword in the Gorge, so Fishlegs was having to fight with his spare sword, which he affectionately called Mr Pointy.

Fishlegs had no parents to give him expensive swordfighting equipment. Fishlegs had found Mr Pointy on the scrapheap at the blacksmiths, so it wasn't really in battle-worthy condition, having a tendency to wobble a little and rattle in its hilt when struck.

Fishlegs was quite a sight, therefore, stumbling round Lardtummy Lo-Watt, trying to defend himself with the wobbly Mr Pointy while the dragon attached to his head squirmed and squealed in alarm, and tried to get as far away as she could from the swords.

There was a nasty moment when Horrorcow became so alarmed that she actually put her paws over his eyes, so Fishlegs could not see Lardtummy's lunges.

'Horrorcow! I can't see!' yelled Fishlegs.

'I'm so sorry,' mooed Horrorcow, 'but it's all so violent and aggressive, can we not do something nice...'

And then, as if things couldn't get any worse, halfway through the fight, Mr Pointy's blade fell out, leaving poor Fishlegs with only the hilt in his hand.

'HA HA HA HA HA HA HA HA HA!' roared the crowd of watching Warriors-to-Be. 'A collapsible blade!'

'Let's see whether we can take that dragon off your head for you, shall we?' sneered Snotlout, flexing his fist and punching it into his hand.

Poor traumatized Horrorcow gave a yowl. 'No violence! I'm a vegetarian!'

HA! HA! HA!

The crowd of Warriors-to-Be closed in on Fishlegs, and all might not have gone well with him if...

'Look out!' yelled Hiccup from above, landing the Windwalker right beside Fishlegs, sending Snotlout and Dogsbreath spinning into the dirt. Fishlegs scrambled on to the Windwalker's back, and they took off.

'Yar! Look, it's that Hiccup who released the Dragon Furious coming to the rescue of his weird friend!' shouted Snotlout.

'Weirdos!' yelled one Grim-bod.

'Freaks!' shouted Very Vicious the Visithug.

A minute later, the two boys were sitting with their friend Camicazi on top of the Second to the Left Tower, having a little breather from swordfighting practice. They were all wearing green swordfighting belts.

Toothless was playing with Camacazi's hunting dragon, Stormfly and One Eye the Sabre-Tooth Driver Dragon, an old friend of Hiccup's, was sitting beside them on the battlements.

'Thanks,' said Fishlegs. 'I had that situation under control, but thanks anyway.'

'Don't mention it,' said Hiccup.

'They're going to kill us when they catch us,' said Fishlegs.

'Well, I'm not exactly the most popular person round here at the minute, so I don't care,' said Hiccup.

It was true.

Ever since it had been revealed that Hiccup freed the Dragon Furious, the Warriors-to-Be had stopped speaking to him. It was as if he was cursed.

Hiccup noticed that even the adult Warriors gave him a wide berth when he approached, getting as far away from him as was physically possible, as if he had some kind of dreadful catching disease.

It was a little depressing.

So what with one thing and another, Hiccup and Fishlegs and Camicazi were spending quite a lot of time keeping out of everyone's way up there on the Second to the Left Tower.

They had a great view of the fighting, leaning over the battlements, peacefully chatting.

'This is not good,' said Fishlegs to Hiccup. 'Alvin seems to have got really, really good at swordfighting.'

They squinted down at the Battle Arena, where hundreds of the Tribesmen were practising their swordfighting in battle bouts.

Alvin the Treacherous was practising against Giant Grim. Giant Grim was a magnificent swordfighter, a FlashMaster Bronze Belt, and a contender to win the whole competition, but Alvin was doing surprisingly well against him, despite his ivory leg.

When they first met him, a couple of years earlier, Alvin wasn't all that good at swordfighting, but he must have been practising hard, and he had really bulked up in the muscle department.

One Eye the Sabre-Tooth Driver Dragon opened his one eye.

'If the horrible human with the hook becomes King of *anything*,' he said, 'I, for one, will be instantly joining the Dragon Rebellion.'

'I don't know why you haven't joined it already,' purred Stormfly naughtily. 'Being such a REVOLUTIONARY and everything,'

'I have a bad leg,' said One Eye with dignity.

'I could beat the lot of them!' said Camicazi, spiritedly making lunges with her sword against imaginary opponents, 'but I'm a bit concerned about my foot...'

Camicazi had had the misfortune to put on her boot two days earlier, only to find a sea urchin had mysteriously found its way into the toe.

OW!!

She had managed to get the prickles out, but was still limping badly.

'It's that witch!' said Fishlegs. 'I know it is! Sea urchins don't throw themselves out of the sea and put themselves into boots all on their own. The witch must have put it there. She wants Alvin to win this swordfighting contest and be the King of the Wilderwest and she's going to try and get rid of everyone who is a good swordfighter and might get in his way.'

It was true.

Odd things had been happening to the good swordfighters all week.

'Remember,' said Fishlegs, 'Helly Thickarm sprained her sword-arm in an arm-wrestling competition with an *Outcast*.'

'And my mother's lucky sword has disappeared...' said Camicazi. 'She doesn't fight half as well without her lucky sword...'

Mogadon the Meathead had developed a stomach complaint that had him rolling around and itching. 'He's eaten something that disagrees with him,' the witch had explained. 'My pink medicine should make him better.'

But the pink medicine made him *worse*. It was all looking very suspicious. The three Heroes squinted down at the Battle Arena.

Watching all of these fights was the crooked figure of the brown-cloaked witch, sitting smoking a pipe in the doorway of her fortune-telling hut.

The fortune-telling hut was a sinister little dwelling squatting behind the Battle Arena like an ugly fat gnome.

The witch had set up shop there. It had a sign outside saying 'Fortunes Told, Futures Improved' written in wobbly capital letters.

People had been visiting the hut all week, to have their fortune told, and to get a home-baked fortune cookie. Everyone who visited the hut came swaggering out, looking very pleased with themselves. Hiccup suspected the witch was telling them ALL that they were going to be the next King of the Wilderwest. 'Ooooooh,' sighed Toothless, sniffing the air. 'Those cookies smell so y-y-yummy...'

Dragons have an extraordinary sense of smell, and he could smell the lovely aroma of freshly baked cookies wafting up from that horrible little hut even from all the way up at the top of the Tower.

The witch seemed to sense they were watching her, and maybe she wasn't so blind after all, for her head tipped upwards and she looked straight at them.

Instinctively, all three of them ducked behind the battlements, three pairs of eyes just peering over the edge.

The witch cackled, and removed her pipe.

'He's doing well, my Alvin, isn't he?' she called up to them. 'He's got a good chance of being Champion of Champions, don't you think? Come and try my cookies some time, duckies, and maybe I can improve your fortunes too…'

She jammed her pipe back in her mouth, and went back to watching the fighting.

'This is not good,' said Fishlegs. 'We can't let Alvin become the next King of the Wilderwest. Who are we going to find who is good enough to beat Alvin?'

'Flashburn!' cried Camicazi excitedly. 'He's the perfect Hero!'

'Yes, but he's completely disappeared,' Fishlegs reminded her. 'Again, I bet you it's that horrible witch. What could she possibly have done with Flashburn AND all those Red Tiger Warriors?'

'Do you think,' Fishlegs paused, and swallowed hard, 'do you think the witch could have KILLED them?'

'She looks nasty enough for anything,' admitted Hiccup. He hoped it wasn't true, but what on earth could she have done with them otherwise?

'I think YOU should win the competition, then, Hiccup,' said Camicazi. 'After all, you have got the King's Things, and Grimbeard's Second-Best Sword and everything...'

Hiccup sighed. 'I'm OK at swordfighting, but I'm way smaller than everyone else. And given that nobody's even TALKING to me right now, I don't think they're going to want me to be the King of the Wilderwest. We just have to find someone else to win and be the King, and then we can give *them* the Things.

'I wonder what is so important about this sword anyway?' Hiccup wondered.

Why is this sword important?

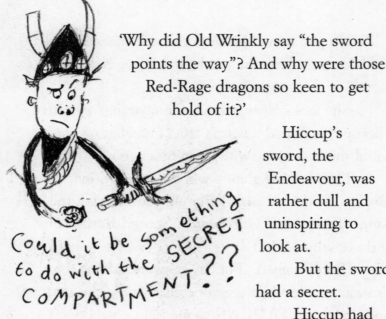

'Why did Old Wrinkly say "the sword points the way"? And why were those Red-Rage dragons so keen to get hold of it?'

Could it be Something to do with the SECRET COMPARTMENT.??

Hiccup's sword, the Endeavour, was rather dull and uninspiring to look at.

But the sword had a secret.

Hiccup had discovered this secret years ago when he first found the sword.*

If you twisted and twisted it, the knob at the end of the sword fell off, to reveal a hidden compartment. There was a will inside, signed by Grimbeard the Ghastly himself, saying that this was his second-best sword, and he left it to his True Heir.

Hiccup unscrewed the secret compartment now, and took out the piece of paper, and re-read it for the hundredth time.

---

* You can read about this in *How to Be a Pirate*.

The Sword Endeavour (OR the Dragonsword")

'↖ Grimbeard's Last Will and Testament is hidden in HERE

But it still gave no clue as to why it might be important to the Red-Rage dragons. Nothing about Rebellions or Kings of the Wilderwest or anything helpful like that.

'HICCUP! WHAT ARE YOU DOING UP THERE? YOU DON'T LOOK LIKE YOU'RE PRACTISING YOUR SWORDFIGHTING! COME DOWN HERE AT ONCE!'

It was the loud bellowing tones of Stoick the Vast, who had won his swordfight, and had spotted his son, up on the Tower. Hiccup jumped, hastily stuffed the piece of paper into the pocket in his waistcoat, thrust his sword into his green swordfighting belt, and leapt on to the Windwalker's back again. The riding-dragon swooped down, a mite sleepily, for it still hadn't recovered from its long winter hibernation.

Hiccup landed beside a sweating Stoick the Vast. 'Yes, Father?'

'Now, Hiccup,' said Stoick sternly. 'You really ought to be practising your swordfighting. You need to put up a good show in this competition, particularly because I think people may be blaming you a little for this whole freeing-the-Dragon-Furious-Red-Rage business. Not me, of course, I understand that it was all a complete accident...'

'Well, it wasn't a *total* accident, Father. I did mean to free him,' admitted Hiccup, honestly, but perhaps a little unwisely. 'In fact, I think we ought to consider freeing ALL the dragons, before the Dragon Furious attacks again.'

'Free all the dragons?!' repeated Stoick the Vast, dangerously quiet. 'What *are* you talking about?'

'Well, Father,' continued Hiccup eagerly, 'if the dragons are already free, then there would be no need for a rebellion, so we can stop the war before it even starts.' Stoick's head was going round and round. He wasn't the brightest barbarian in the business, and this was way too complicated for him.

'SILENCE!' roared Stoick. 'Enough of this freeing nonsense! You've got us all in enough trouble as it is. And I don't want you hanging out with that Fish-eggs-with-a-dragon-on-his-head boy any more either, you're making us look ridiculous!'

'It's not Fishlegs's fault he's got a dragon on his head. We're trying to get it down, it just won't COME down.'

Stoick struggled to keep his temper. 'I understand, Hiccup, but people are already looking at you suspiciously, and if you wander around with a runty looking boy with a large dragon attached to his head people are going to start thinking that you're ODD and *odd* is not something that people like around here.'

'We've been through this before, Father,' said Hiccup. 'Fishlegs is my friend and he stands by me so I have to stand by him—'

'THAT WAS BEFORE YOU BROUGHT SHAME ON ALL THIS TRIBE BY FREEING THE DRAGON FURIOUS!' It came out harsher than Stoick had intended. Hiccup was quiet, shocked.

'You have to grow up, Hiccup,' said Stoick, more calmly. 'You are my Heir, and you need to put away childish things and show a little leadership. Practise your swordfighting, son. Enough talk about freeing dragons and what-not. Just practise your swordfighting and get a good belt, that's all I ask.'

And Stoick stomped off.

'I think you should show off your swordfighting a little LESS, Father,' said Hiccup dejectedly. 'The witch is getting rid of people who are any good.'

But Stoick had already left, and he wasn't in the mood to listen to this excellent advice.

Flamehuffers

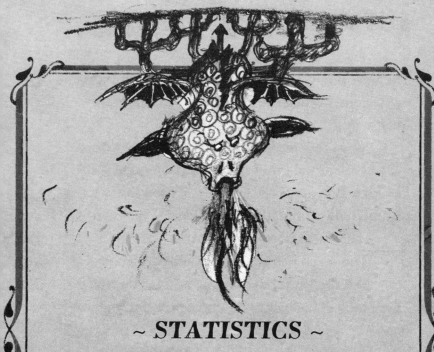

~ STATISTICS ~

FEAR FACTOR: 3
ATTACK: 3
SPEED: 4
SIZE: 3
DISOBEDIENCE: 7

Flamehuffers are mischievous,
unpredictable little creatures who like
to cause trouble. They are astonishing
ventriloquists, and are very good at
mimicking human voices.

7. FORTUNES TOLD, FUTURES IMPROVED

The next day, Giant Grim came down with the same mysterious stomach complaint as Mogadon the Meathead.

'Wasn't Giant Grim the one who was sword-fighting Alvin the other day and doing quite well?' said Fishlegs. 'And wasn't it him who visited the witch's fortune-telling hut later on that day?'

That was indeed Giant Grim.

'The witch has got him…' hissed Fishlegs.

And then two days after that, Hardbottomed HighHat lost his lucky hat, and refused to fight at all unless he found it again.

'The witch has got him…' whispered Fishlegs.

Young Aggie Ardache, Longlegs Lardyguts, Rubella the Rude, all wonderful swordfighters, fell victim to the same weird problem that Camicazi had. They put on their boots, only to find a sea urchin nestling in the toe, and were limping around the castle as a result.

'The witch has got them…' hissed Fishlegs.

Daddy, Mummy and baby sea urchins..

'Have you ever heard
of a whole herd
of homing sea
urchins nesting
in shoes?'

Hiccup
begged
his father
to pretend
to be worse at
swordfighting.

'Please, Father,
it's the witch, she's
getting rid of
anyone who
is any good...
I've seen her
watching you in the Battle Arena... And for Thor's
sake, whatever you do, don't visit her horrible fortune-
telling hut...'

But Stoick would not listen. He was too proud.

'Nonsense!' roared Stoick the Vast. 'I will visit
whoever I like, Hiccup! I've spoken to several people
who say the witch has already improved their futures,

*flocks of homing
sea urchins nesting in
shoes...*

147

and I hear that her cookies are delicious!'

But when the next lot of brilliant swordfighters went down with weird illnesses and minor accidents involving sea urchins, even the stupidest of the Vikings began to get worried.

Wouldn't you?

The Battle Arena was awash with spotty, itching swordfighters, limping and clutching their tummies, and poor superstitious people like Hardbottomed HighHat unable to fight at all, just roaming the castle looking for his lucky hat.

The Outcasts were the only Tribe that seemed unaffected, practising quietly with each other, on the edge of the arena.

No longer were there the merry parties, the practising late into the night. Once again, the castle seemed the haunted place to which they first came.

'Let us leave this cursed spot!' cried Mogadon the Meathead, in the Banqueting Hall that evening. 'Too many bad things are happening. And it is too risky here, anyway. What if the rebel dragons were to attack? They could wipe us all out in one go!'

The witch was sitting quietly, poking the fire.

'Oh, but you cannot leave,' said the witch, her

voice as sweet as poison. 'A promise is a promise, if it is made in blood.

A promise is a promise, if it is made in BLOOD...

No, you must stay here a little while, as you pledged, and fight to be the Champion of Champions on the turning of the Year...'

The Vikings turned to the Eldest Elder, and anxiously he raked up his white hair until it stood all on end. He took out the piece of paper that the Chiefs had all signed up to, and checked it. Oh dear. 'A promise *is* a promise,' admitted the Eldest Elder reluctantly, 'if it is made in blood.'

That was a quiet feast in the Banqueting Hall that night, with no one talking to his neighbour.

No one walked about on their own; they went about in big groups, with weapons drawn. No one ate a piece of food before their own dragons had tasted it. They checked very, very carefully inside their gloves and shoes.

The torches stayed burning all through the night in the dormitories. Each Tribe posted sentries that paced the room while the others slept, to watch out for danger sneaking in at the doors and the windows.

And then, only one day before the swordfighting competition, all of Hiccup's worries came true...

The witch got Stoick the Vast.

Not with a nasty tummyache, or even a sea urchin in the shoe. No, it was far worse than that.

Stoick the Vast disappeared entirely.

Just like Flashburn and his forty Warriors.

It happened like this.

On New Year's Eve, Hiccup was awoken in the middle of the night.

After three weeks of swordfighting practice, morn, noon and night, Hiccup was so exhausted he had to be shaken awake, and when he opened his

sleepy eyes a very, very sick feeling came to his
stomach as he realized that standing all about his bed
were seven of Stoick's most important Warriors, flares
in their hands, and they were arguing fiercely.

'This is ridiculous!' fumed Baggybum the
Beerbelly. 'This is a national emergency! You can't put
this boy in charge! He isn't even a proper Warrior yet.
He's not ready. He may NEVER be ready. Let's face
it, nobody dared tell Stoick, but he's a bit of a little
weirdo. Look at his arms, like two pieces of spaghetti!
I should be the temporary Chief, as Stoick's younger
brother!'

'Hiccup will become a full Warrior tomorrow,'
said Gobber the Belch heavily. 'And we must give the
boy a chance. By report he fought bravely and cleverly
on the Angry Face, leading them all to victory...
Perhaps he will do the same for us...'

'LUCK!' roared Baggybum. 'Sheer luck! We can't
make this boy the Chief because he was the one who
set free the Dragon Furious! We all know that. None
of the other Warriors will even speak to him. The other
Tribes think he may be cursed...'

'The setting free of the Dragon Furious was
an accident. I had plenty of accidents when I was

151

thirteen,' argued Gobber the Belch.

(Hiccup had no idea that Gobber would stand up for him in this way, and he was rather touched.)

'None of this matters,' said Nobber Nobrains. 'Hiccup is the Heir, so he is the Stand-in-Chief.'

Back and forth the Warriors argued, until at last they voted, four against three, that Hiccup should be the Stand-in-Chief.

'But if it all goes horribly wrong,' grumbled Baggybum the Beerbelly, 'and trust me, it will with this weirdo in charge, I will take over.'

Hiccup swallowed hard, white as paper. 'What is going on? Why do I have to be the Stand-in-Chief? Where is my father? Is he ill? Is he wounded?'

'Your father has gone missing,' said Nobber Nobrains. 'He went out earlier this evening, he said he had someone to visit, and he has never returned. You are the Chief for the moment. What are your orders?'

They were all looking at him.

Beyond the circle of the seven men, all the Hooligans were awake now, and looking at him.

Snotlout gave Hiccup his meanest most spiteful look, and whispered, 'Go on cousin, CRY... Blub for your father, like the baby you are...'

A Chief puts his own personal feelings aside for the good of the Tribe…

Stoick's words floated through Hiccup's brain.

A Chief must show no fear, no worry… A Chief is a leader first, and a man second…

Hiccup stood up, and buckled on his green swordfighting belt, trying to keep his hands steady.

He looked Gobber the Belch straight in the eye.

Hiccup's thoughts were shrieking:

Where is he? He must have gone to visit that horrible witch, but what has she done with him? She couldn't have **KILLED** *him, could she?*

But he kept his face calm.

'Search the castle,' ordered Hiccup.

Gobber the Belch and the six other Elders bowed, three of them furiously and reluctantly.

The Hooligans had the castle all in uproar, searching for Stoick, going through every chamber in the school, waking everybody up.

But they found no trace of Stoick.

'Search the witch hut, too,' ordered Hiccup.

'But, Hiccup,' protested Nobber Nobrains, 'the witch is an Elder! (*And she's* **SUPER** *scary.*) It's an insult… You can't search the hut of an Elder…'

'Search the hut,' repeated Hiccup.

KNOCK! KNOCK! KNOCK! on the witch's door.

'I am so sorry, Madam,' bowed a deeply embarrassed Baggybum. 'We have come to search your hut... Orders of our temporary Chieftain...'

'Unconventional, and a bit of an insult,' purred the witch, her hooded snake eyes looking, if anything, a little amused, 'but of course, be my guest.'

She knew we were coming...

Seven Hooligan Warriors squeezed into the little fortune-telling hut, and searched it very thoroughly indeed. They found nothing, of course, and had to come out red-faced and apologize to the witch again in front of all the other Tribes.

'I forgive you,' smiled Excellinor, 'because your Stand-in-Chief is so young and inexperienced, he does not know how rude he is being. But he will learn...' she said grimly, turning her white sightless head like a clockwork thing in the direction of Hiccup. 'Oh yes,' (*what* a threat she could get in that soft voice) 'he will learn...'

'You see,' a scarlet Baggybum the Beerbelly spat savagely to Nobber Nobrains as they stomped away from the hut, through the whispering crowds, 'he's making us look ridiculous already!'

The Hooligans carried on their search for the whole of the next day.

But there was no sign of Stoick the Vast.

Hiccup had a sleepless night that New Year's Eve, worrying about what might have happened to his father. And he was still awake when the sun rose on New Year's Day. It was a glorious cold winter's morning, with not a cloud in the sky or a breath of wind, perfect weather for a swordfighting competition.

where is he?
where is he?
where is HE?

WHere could he BE?

♪ ♪ ♪
"Toothless — ♪
is a scaredy-cat..."
♪

At breakfast time, Toothless and Stormfly paid their own secret visit to the witch's hut.

Toothless and Stormfly would do anything for FOOD.

The delicious smell of the fortune cookies had been tempting them for weeks, so when Stormfly discovered a small hole in the back of the hut, she dared Toothless to squeeze through and steal some of the cookies.

'N-n-no,' said Toothless, looking at the hole.

He was scared of the witch.

'Toothless not hungry.' His stomach gave a big rumble.

'The witch isn't in there,' said Stormfly. 'I saw her go to the Banqueting Hall for breakfast.'

'Y-y-you're quite sure,' said Toothless, 'there's NO WITCH in there?'

'Quite sure. I'll keep a look-out in case she comes back,' said Stormfly.

Stormfly batted her eyelashes. Stormfly was a Mood-Dragon. Mood-Dragons are chameleons, and now she turned a lovely pale violet as she cooed: 'You're such a brave, wonderful dragon, Toothless, and you're just the perfect size to fit through that hole, I'm too big...'

'No,' said Toothless, for once standing his ground.

Stormfly looked through her lashes at him. 'Toothless is a scaredy-cat...' she sang.

'Toothless NOT a scaredy-cat!' howled Toothless.

'Yes he i-i-i-is...' sang Stormfly.

Toothless hovered around the hole, circling it furiously, gathered up all his courage and squeezed through it.

"Toothless NOT a scaredy-cat."

One minute later he shot
out again, all in a tizzy, like
he was being pursued by
wolves, his mouth and
talons full of fortune
cookies.

He dropped some
at Stormfly's feet, and flew
off with the rest to find Hiccup.

Hiccup and Fishlegs and Camicazi were standing
outside the Banqueting Hall, joining the queues to get
in. Hiccup was hoping that the breakfast would wake
him up, for he was feeling very rough after his sleepless
night, when Toothless landed on his shoulder.

'What are you eating, Toothless?' Hiccup
scolded. 'I hope that's something edible, and not a
key or a bracelet or something.'

Toothless opened up his claw to show Hiccup the
fortune cookies.

Hiccup gave a gasp when he realized what they
were, and hurried round the corner so that no one else
would see them.

'Where did you find these, Toothless?'

In each fortune cookie there was a piece of

paper sticking out. Written on the pieces of
paper were the words, 'YOU are the King
of the Wilderwest.'

Toothless gobbled up another one, paper and
all, before Hiccup could stop him.

Eventually, he spoke through a mouthful of
cookie, spraying crumbs in all directions.

'He's in the witch's h-h-hut,' said Toothless.

Hiccup jumped.

'Who is?'

'Your father,' replied Toothless.

'How do you know?' asked Hiccup.

'His s-s-sword was on the table,' explained
Toothless. 'And there was a big h-h-hat...'

'Hardbottomed HighHat's hat?' asked Hiccup.

Toothless nodded.

He gobbled up three more of the fortune cookies
before Hiccup could tell him not to.

I knew it, thought Hiccup. *I knew it, I knew it, I
knew it...*

Hiccup ran around the corner again and looked in the door of the Banqueting Hall.

He could see the witch, shrouded in her brown cloak, eating at her place by the fire. He had at least five minutes, he reckoned, before she finished and got back to the hut.

'Where are you going? You're going to that witch's fortune-telling hut, aren't you?' hissed Fishlegs, running after him. 'You're crazy! She'll kill you if she finds you in there!' Fishlegs whirled his arms around like windmills. 'At least go in there with somebody else, like a whole search party!'

'I have to find my father,' said Hiccup. 'I can't ask anyone else, they already think they've searched the hut. As soon as we KNOW my father's in there, we can get reinforcements. The witch is in the Banqueting Hall, we'll just search it very, very quickly before she comes out...'

'Mmmff!' said Toothless, red in the face. He had something very important to say, but he couldn't say it with his mouth full of three fortune cookies all at once. He tried to swallow them, but there were too many of them...

'She's going to catch you, I know she is!' cried

Fishlegs. 'Oh, brother, this is awful… I know this is going to turn out like it always does, with some dreadful surprise, or us up to our armpits in Poisonous Piffleworms or Brainpickers or something.'

'You don't have to come too,' Hiccup pointed out.

'Of course I have to come too!' moaned Fishlegs. 'I'm your sidekick aren't I? And sometimes you need me, not often, but you do. And imagine if that was the one time I wasn't there, I'd feel awful…'

'I think it's a brilliant idea,' said Camicazi, running along beside them. 'And you really need a burglar like me if you're going to thoroughly search that old hag's hut. It's got to be a professional job. Witches are excellent at hiding things. But they can't hide things from ME, I have magic fingers and I'm the best hunter in the Archipelago.'

'MMMMFFF! MMMMFF!! MFFFF!!!' said Toothless, desperately munching at the fortune cookies, and trying to flap in front of them to stop them.

Camicazi put on her black gloves while running along, not as fast as she normally did because she still had a pronounced limp.

'I will go through this hut with a fine-tooth comb, I am telling you.' She took a comb from her pocket, raising her finger in the air. 'I will search it like a Sniffer crossed with a bloodhound crossed with a wolf. I will leave no witchtooth unturned, no sock unsniffed, no cauldron uninvestigated. When I am done, I will know everything. That witch will have absolutely no secrets left.'

They stopped outside the hut.

It was a very small hut.

Very small indeed.

And it was spooky.

'I do not BELIEVE it,' whispered Fishlegs.

He had just noticed that between the wobbly sign saying, Fortunes Told, Futures Improved, and the sign in smaller letters below, LOST PROPERTY, there were letters carved over the door in a handwriting he recognized. Letters carved long ago, by a man long dead, a dreadful old pirate with a wicked sense of humour.

The letters read: BEWARE YE WHO ENTER HERE.

'Grimbeard the Ghastly! This must have been his hut! Owowowowowow!' (as Horrorcow gripped her claws) 'This means that there will be some horrible surprise… some booby-trap… some disaster…'

'This means,' said Hiccup, 'that we're getting warm.'

All three of them drew their swords.

'MMMMMFFFFF!! MMMMMMFFFFF!!! MMMMMFFFFF!!!!'

Toothless was going crazy, mouth full of fortune cookies, unable to speak, but throwing himself in front of the door, trying to stop them from going in.

'Don't worry, Toothless,' said Hiccup soothingly. 'We won't go in for long, and Stormfly will keep a look out for the witch, won't you Stormfly?'

Stormfly, who had finished her cookies, was loitering by the door.

She nodded. 'Of course I will,' she said, 'I'll just pop in with you for a second to get some more of those cookies, they're absolutely delicious…'

'MMMMMMFFFF! MFFFFF!!! MFFFFF!'

Toothless was turning cartwheels in the air, he was so hysterical to tell them something important.

Hiccup took out the key-that-opens-all-locks.

'Oh, I can't look,' moaned Fishlegs, putting his hands over his eyes.

Fortunes
Told
Futures
Improved

BEWARE HE WHO ENTER

LOST
PROPERTY

Hiccup opened the door.

8. OH FOR THOR'S SAKE, OF COURSE THEY SHOULDN'T SEARCH THAT FORTUNE-TELLING HUT! HAVE YOU NOT READ ANY OF HICCUP'S MEMOIRS BEFORE?

As soon as they opened the door, they regretted it.

A crooked little room, so dark that they blinked and struggled to see, and it took a moment or two to peer into the blackness as they stumbled forward, Toothless protesting desperately and trying to pull Hiccup out again by grabbing the back of his waistcoat with his talons.

And as their eyes adjusted to the very faint light of a dying fire and a couple of Slugbulbs drowning pathetically in a bowl of water, in one ghastly moment the implications of the room burst upon them.

Cobwebs everywhere. A mess of bottles and potions, and bits of meat. Maps and scribblings and decaying paper on the walls with great complicated charts and family trees splatted with what looked like

blood. Things drying on washing lines that might be fingernails or bits of hair. A game of chess on a table with one leg propped up by books. A large dark cupboard in the corner of the room. A great cauldron on a dimly flickering fire… And in the centre of it all… In the centre of it all…

A brown-cloaked figure, sitting in a chair, as if it had been waiting for them.

Oh, they turned as soon as they saw what was in that hut. They turned and tried to run, scrabbled for the door they had just come through on desperate legs with hearts beating quick and a dreadful sick feeling in their dropping stomachs…

… but to no avail.

A great wind came from behind them
as the door was slammed SHUT by
unseen hands.

And it was too late.

They were trapped.

'I thought you'd never
arrive, Hiccup Horrendous
Haddock the Third. I've
been waiting for you
for ages,' drawled the
brown-cloaked figure,
and it slowly pulled
back its
hood.

It was the witch.

'Mmmf GULP!'

At last Toothless managed to swallow the last mouthful of the fortune cookies, and he squealed, 'YOU S-S-SEE! TOOTHLESS TRY TO TELL YOU! THE WITCH IS STILL IN HERE! MUST BE SOMEBODY ELSE IN THE B-B-BANQUETING HALL!'

Toothless dived down Hiccup's shirt, whirling round his stomach, and ending up somewhere in the hollow of Hiccup's back, trembling.

The witch smiled.

She spoke as if she understood Dragonese.

'Yes, one of my Outcast friends is at this very moment sitting in the Banqueting Hall, wearing one of my brown cloaks. You see, I have more than one.'

She was upright, but hunched over like she was used to a smaller space, turning a great sand-glass over and over in terribly wrinkled hands. She was still so painfully white, so drained of colour, that Hiccup could hardly bear to look at her. Bones were so visible under her skin that it was like staring straight at a skull, tapping fingernails tipped with iron.

Tap, tap, tap on the sand-glass.

Tick-tock, tick-tock in Hiccup's pocket.

A scary sight, the witch Excellinor.

'It is so nice to have you here all on your own, my children,' cooed the wicked witch, 'without all those horrid muscly grown-ups. Would you like a cookie?'

She pointed to a large basket of delicious smelling cookies, sitting on the table.

'No?' she purred. 'Then what can I do to entertain you? Do you play chess? I may have to warn you that I am very, very good…'

Beside the chess game on the table there was a high hat, Stoick's sword, a cigar case that Hiccup recognized as belonging to UG the Uglithug, and Flashburn's red necktie.

'But I am in the middle of a game. Or perhaps,' said the witch, her voice as sweet as poison,

In the corner was a locked cupboard.

'perhaps you have come to have your
fortunes told, and your futures improved?'

The three Vikings looked at her, mute
with terror, like three little mice that had been
cornered by a viper.

'Or maybe you have lost something?'

'What have you done with my father, you

horrible witch?' asked Hiccup, getting straight to the point, and gesturing at his father's sword.

'Well now, my ducky darling, fathers are rather overrated I feel,' said the witch. 'But I love a guessing game. What do you think I have done with him? Your Warriors searched the room earlier, and found nothing.'

'Did they look in the cupboard?' asked Hiccup.

There was a large dark cupboard in the corner of the room.

'The cupboard is locked,' replied the witch, 'and no one knows where the key is.'

And yet there **WAS** *a key, hanging round the witch's neck.*

'It was careless of you to lose

your father. But perhaps I can help you find him again. Let's play a game of hide-and-seek, and the prize shall be your father. If *you* find something for ME, well then, perhaps I can find your father for YOU. If you fail to find the Thing I want, well,' the witch shrugged her shoulders, 'then you father shall remain unfound...' A very, very nasty smile came over the witch's skeleton face. 'FOR EVER.'

'That's not a very nice game,' said Camicazi.

'I'm not a very nice person,' said the witch.

'What do you want me to find?' asked Hiccup.

'I want you to find me the Lost Crown of the Wilderwest.'

'What makes you think that I shall be able to find this Crown, if you haven't been able to find it yourself?' asked Hiccup.

'Just a feeling,' said the witch, looking at him with acute dislike. 'Look at you, you horrible little boy, you're absolutely *festooned* with the King's Lost Things, without even trying. They're *throwing* themselves at you...'

The witch was hissing like a serpent now, and she pointed, one by one, to the Things. 'You have six of the Things already. The Roman shield, the ticking-

172

thing, the arrow-from-the land-that-does-not-exist, the key-that-opens-all-locks, the heart's stone and the second-best sword... You're just showing off, really, aren't you?'

'I didn't mean to get these things,' protested Hiccup. 'It was all an accident.'

'There are no accidents,' said the witch grimly.

Why did people keep saying that?

'It's as if those Things were looking for you,' said the witch, 'as if you were some horrible Hiccup-shaped magnet, stealing my darling Alvin's destiny. Well, now I am back, I can burgle that luck right back again, you just see if I don't.

'You are going to give these six Things to me,' cooed the witch.

'I most certainly am not!' declared Hiccup.

'Not now, but eventually you will,' the witch assured him. 'NOW you will find me the Lost Crown of the Wilderwest. Bring me the Crown, and I will give you back your father.'

'So where do we look for this Crown then?' asked Hiccup.

There was a cauldron in the middle of the room, hanging from a tripod over a fire. The witch bent down, and moved the fire, burning in a brazier, to reveal a trapdoor. She opened the trapdoor to reveal a well underneath.

'Oh, for Thor's sake,' moaned Fishlegs. 'What did I tell you? We'll be up to our armpits in Poisonous Piffleworms before we know WHERE we are...'

The witch giggled, and it was like stones rattling in a tin.

'Down below this room is a dungeon. The only way *in* is down this well... And that, my dears, as far as I know, is the only way out.'

'And what is in this dungeon?' asked Hiccup.

'Well it's either nothing dangerous at all,' grinned the witch. 'Or it's Riproarers, Brainpickers, Death and Darkness. Somewhere down in that maze of tunnels is the Fire Pit. And somewhere in that Fire Pit is the Lost Crown of the Wilderwest...'

'And being Grimbeard, he has probably booby-trapped the place in the most fiendish way,' groaned Fishlegs. 'Oh, Hiccup, we really can't do this one...'

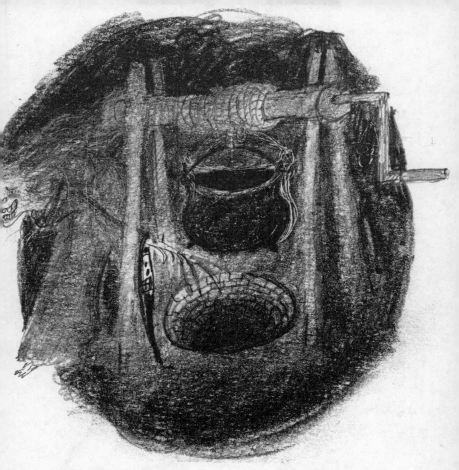

The witch looked at them, her head tilted to
one side.

'So... do you choose to play my game or not?'

'You have no sword,' said Hiccup slowly. 'There
are three of us, and you are an old woman. I could
just overpower you and open that cupboard with
my key.'

175

'You *could*,' said the witch playfully. 'But my fingernails are poisoned with the deadliest of poisons known to man. If I were to scratch you, and one DROP of this poison were to get into your blood, you would die a long and agonizing death. So I wouldn't do that if I were you.'

The witch twirled her iron fingernails. When Hiccup looked closer, each iron-tipped nail had been dipped in a dark purple substance a little like ink, and a lot like death itself.

'These nails,' said the witch, 'are as full of death as an apothecary's shop. I tried them on the rats, and the rats didn't like them, not one bit.' She

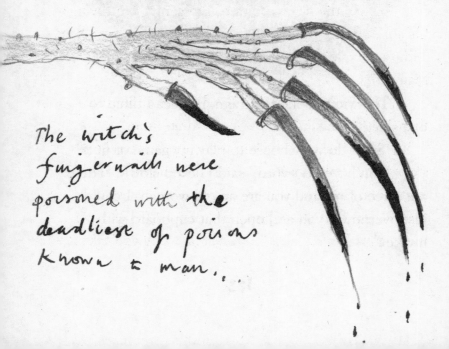

The witch's fingernails were poisoned with the deadliest of poisons known to man...

gestured to the corner, where a line of rats were lying with their stiff little legs frozen in the air.

Oh the children shivered, yes they did, to see those little corpses all in a row.

'And it might be that your father is not inside that cupboard after all. I could be ly-y-y-yinnngg!' sang the witch delightedly. 'Isn't this a great game?'

'Wonderful,' said Hiccup politely. 'And how do I know that you are telling the truth about the Crown being down that well?'

'You do-o-o-on't!' sang the witch. 'I could be lying about that to-o-o-o-o! I could just be trying to get you out of the w-a-a-a-ayyyy!

'That's the whole point of the game. Am I lying? Or am I speaking the truth? Play a round of Liar Dice with me, while you decide, and we'll see how lucky you really are...'

In her bony hands she took the dice, poured them in the shaker, and rattled it three times.

'So ho!' she cried. And then, 'Let's see now,' as she set the shaker on the table, lifted the lid a mere crack, and peered inside greedily.

'Ooh, four skulls and one bone... Who'd have thought it? I'm a lucky, lucky woman. Will you take it,

Liar Dice and Shaker

Hiccup the Third, or will you call my bluff?'

Liar Dice is a game of luck and wits.

If Hiccup took the hand he would have to beat it with his next throw. Her face was a mask.

Was it truth or was it a lie?

'I'll take it...' said Hiccup at last.

'A wise decision,' nodded the witch. 'But now you have to beat my throw...'

She passed the shaker over.

Hiccup opened the lid.

She spoke the truth... this time.

Four skulls and one bone.

Hiccup picked up the dice with the bone on it, threw it back into the shaker, and without looking to see where it landed, he passed the shaker back to the witch.

'Five skulls,' said Hiccup Horrendous Haddock the Third.

He got to his feet.

The witch and the boy had been talking about more than a game of Liar Dice.

'I'll go and get this Crown for you,' said Hiccup, 'because I have no other option. For if I do not, you will kill both my father and myself.'

'Corr-ect,' said the witch.

Hiccup sighed. He checked the ticking-thing. 'This means we only have three hours to find the Crown and get back in time for the swordfighting competition.'

'Corr-ect,' said the witch again. 'We'll miss you so much if you're late...'

'And if I bring back the Crown, you set me free, of course,' said Hiccup casually.

'Of course,' cooed the witch. 'Word of a Treacherous.'

'HA!' said Fishlegs. 'We've heard that one before…'

'I need my friends to come with me,' said Hiccup.

'Why?' said the witch suspiciously.

Because if I leave them here with you, you will kill them.

'Because I never do Hero Work without them,' said Hiccup. 'Camicazi here is a burglar of some distinction. And Fishlegs here is… half-man, half-dragon. We call him… Tracker Boy.'

'Woof,' yelped Fishlegs, to back him up.

'As you wish,' shrugged the witch. 'In you pop, my duckies. Good luck.'

So Hiccup and Fishlegs and Camicazi climbed into the swinging cauldron, which was still a little hot from the fire, and *clank, clank, clank*, the witch took hold of the tripod's handle and reeled them down into the bowels of the earth.

'Come on, Stormfly!' called Camicazi, just in time, for they had nearly forgotten the beautiful Mood-dragon, who had been quietly munching her way through the basket of fortune cookies while this conversation was going on.

When she got to the end of the chain, the witch looked down the hole with a grunt of delight.

Then she went down on all fours and crept back to the table, and took off the lid of the shaker to see what Hiccup had thrown in the dice game.

'*Five skulls...*' whispered the witch to herself, angrily. 'He is a lucky, clever little rat, Thor rot him...

'Well, he'll need all the luck and the cleverness he can get down there, he will,' she added, with savage satisfaction. 'The game isn't over yet, not by a long way.'

And she hobbled back to her chess game.

Liar Dice

skulls   ships   helmets   fish   dragons

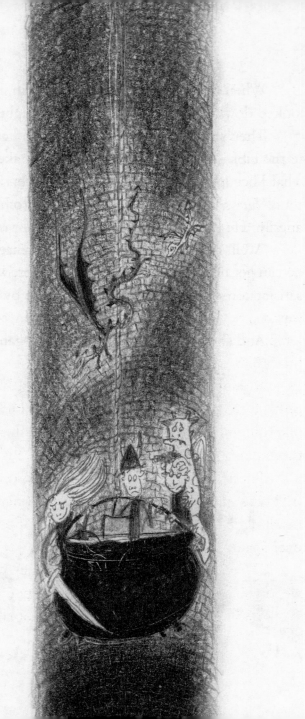

9. GOING DOWN

The three of them sat side by side on the cauldron, six hands on the chain in the middle.

Within sixty seconds, they had descended into total blackness, apart from the eyebeams of Toothless and Horrorcow and Stormfly.

After five minutes they were still going down.

'OW, OW, OW, OW, OW,' whispered Fishlegs, as Horrorcow's talons tightened. 'I never thought I'd say this, but I even feel sorry for Alvin, having her for a mother. Do you think that wicked old skeleton really has Stoick trapped in her cupboard?'

'I think so,' Hiccup whispered back. 'But it's very difficult to tell, because she's such a good liar. The one thing I'm sure she was telling the truth about was those poisoned fingernails.'

Hiccup shivered a little, for he was so very frightened for Stoick. 'My father'll be all right... he'll be all right...' Hiccup repeated to himself over and over again, for comfort.

'This is so annoying,' said Camicazi. 'At this rate we're going to be really late for the competition.'

'HA!' spluttered Fishlegs. 'We're not going to

be late for the competition, Camicazi, we're going to miss it entirely. And do you know why we are going to miss it?' he said in his chattiest voice. 'We are going to miss it because we are going to be dead. You're right, being dead is always annoying.' For morale was already low, and sinking lower and lower the further they sank down the well.

This was already a really long way down. How much further were they going to go? Hiccup looked up. The circle of dim firelight that was the well-head was now no bigger than a pin.

Fishlegs's hands were sweaty on the iron chain. He tried to peer down into the blackness below. 'What do you know about Brainpickers, Hiccup?'

'Well,' whispered Hiccup, 'I know they feed on peoples' brains by sucking them out through their ears.'

'Lovely,' said Fishlegs, shakily, 'and I suppose you are right as rain after that little operation?'

'Even Lardtummy Lo-Watt can't function without some sort of brain, Fishlegs,' said Hiccup. 'Although they're quite small, Brainpickers are one of the most feared dragons in the Archipelago. Even Seadragonus Giganticus Maximus are scared of them, because nobody likes the idea of having their brain sucked out.'

Fishlegs swallowed hard. 'And what other dragons are we likely to meet?'

'Well, the cave dragons are a pretty nasty bunch down here,' said Hiccup. 'Hopefully they'll all still be hibernating. But Grimbeard has found the most dangerous place on the planet to hide his Crown. There's Riproarers – horrible creatures that dribble and scream. They tear you limb from limb if they get you. And then there's Breathquenchers (a bit like gigantic pythons), and Burrowing Slitherfangs of course... and Stickyworms – they trap you in a web and cover you in slime before they eat you...'

But Hiccup wasn't able to finish the long list of particularly unpleasant and dangerous dragons that might inhabit the dungeons of the Flashburn School of Swordfighting.

Because the cauldron in the well at last reached its dungeon destination with a THUMP! so violent that the cauldron tipped sideways and the three young Vikings spilled out on to the dungeon floor.

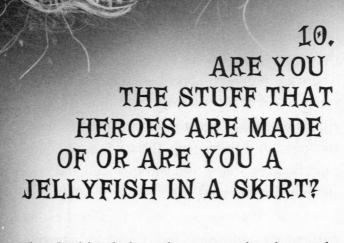

10.
ARE YOU THE STUFF THAT HEROES ARE MADE OF OR ARE YOU A JELLYFISH IN A SKIRT?

They had landed in a large cave chamber, with walls of ice, the air breathtakingly cold. It was lit up by Glow-worms, and Slugbulbs, and the odd blinking light of an Electricsticky. An Electricsticky is a bit like an Electricsquirm, but it clings to cave walls with a sticky substance it secretes out of its bottom. DO NOT PICK ONE UP –

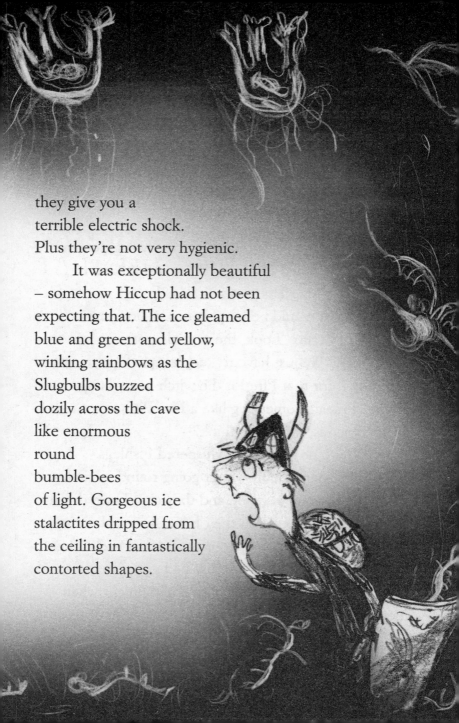

they give you a
terrible electric shock.
Plus they're not very hygienic.

It was exceptionally beautiful
– somehow Hiccup had not been
expecting that. The ice gleamed
blue and green and yellow,
winking rainbows as the
Slugbulbs buzzed
dozily across the cave
like enormous
round
bumble-bees
of light. Gorgeous ice
stalactites dripped from
the ceiling in fantastically
contorted shapes.

There were numerous different tunnels leading away from the chamber, and a strange noise like a distant rumble, or could it be roaring?

'How interesting,' whispered Hiccup slowly. 'The tunnels are made of ice – they must be lava tubes – or perhaps they're the old tunnels of a Giant Burrowing Slitherfang.'

'You always get interested at really frightening moments,' moaned Fishlegs. 'What if that Giant Burrowing Slitherfang was still alive?'

'Then it would be roughly ten million years old,' said Hiccup. 'Look, the cave dragons are still hibernating. We just have to keep as quiet as we can, and search for that Fire Pit the witch was talking about. I mean, something like a Fire Pit has got to be pretty obvious, don't you think?'

'Where do we start?' whispered Fishlegs.

They spent the first hour going round in circles.

The tunnels were icy, and they could race down them at quite a speed on their bone skates, shooting through tunnels that looped in and out of each other like a web spun by a spider that had gone crazy.

They had one slightly alarming moment when they entered a cavern that was dripping with dragons

of all shapes
and sizes, over every
rock and hanging from the
ceiling in thick clusters, like
bats.

But Hiccup
was right, they were
all still hibernating,
and the three
companions
backed out of
the chamber
without being
detected.

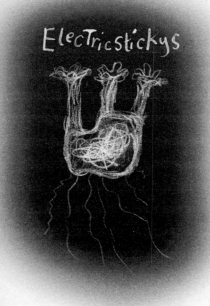

ElectricStickys

However an hour later, they were back where they started, at the cauldron and the well, with no sign of a Fire Pit.

'OK,' whispered Hiccup, 'this is going to be harder than I thought. These tunnels go on for ever.'

He checked the ticking-thing. 'We only have two hours left...'

But Stormfly had shot ahead, and spotted something.

'Look!' she screeched, zooming back to them in a glorious golden swoop. She had spied something with her sharp yellow eyes. 'There seems to be a trail of some sort of chain at the edge of the corridor. Should we follow it instead of going randomly round in circles? Although that is fun.'

'I saw that!' crowed Toothless. 'I s-s-saw the chain too! You saw it first, Stormfly,' he added hurriedly, 'because you're BRILLIANT, but I saw that t-t-too!'

The chain looked like it was going somewhere... unlike themselves.

It started right back at the cauldron tipped on its side, and snaked as far as they could see along the corridor ahead.

'OK,' said Hiccup, for want of anything better to do. 'Everyone draw their swords, and let's follow the chain.'

Slugbulbs

Hiccup picked up the
chain as they went along,
thinking that a piece of chain
might come in handy (better
than rope, of course, because
it wasn't flammable) and they
followed it to see where it
led, up tunnels and round
bends. And then Stormfly
dived round the corner,
disappeared and gave a
muffled scream, only dwarfed
by the scream Toothless gave
as he flew round to save her.

But by the time the
other three got round the
corner in a right panicky
hurry to rescue both dragons,
the drama was over. Stormfly
was sniffing, 'Huh, only a
human,' and Toothless was
squeaking, 'I knew that!'
and swooping nearer to
investigate.

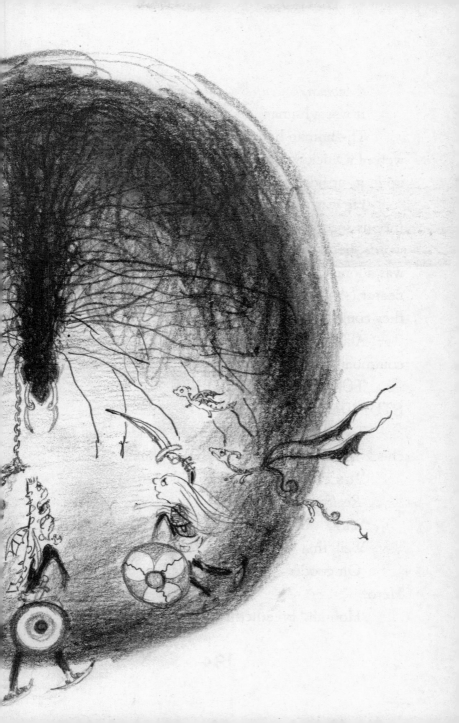

A human?

It was a human in a predicament.

The human had skated right into the invisible web of a Stickyworm, and he had become all tangled up in it, upside-down.

He was whispering something at them, in a hissy, furious sort of way, but it was difficult to make out the words, because he was whispering upside-down, and he was a long way down the corridor. But as they moved nearer (skating quite slowly because they were wary) they could hear what he was saying.

And then as they got nearer still, it was a continual tirade of abuse.

'FOOLS! IGNORAMUSES! STUPIDISSIMOS!'

Toothless flew ahead, turned upside-down to check who it was, and flew back to them.

'It's Flashburn,' said Toothless.

'Really?'

'Yup,' said Toothless, 'it's definitely him.'

Well, that improved their mood, no end!

'Oh goodee,' sang Camicazi. 'It's the perfect Hero!'

'Hoorah,' breathed Fishlegs.

Hiccup felt a great lifting of the heart.

Their luck had turned. This was just what they needed. Flashburn was the kind of brilliant Hero who could find the Crown for them, and if they could only get him back up to the surface he could beat Alvin in the swordfighting competition standing on his head...

Flashburn didn't seem very pleased to see them though.

'NUMBSKULLS! ONE-CELLED JELLYFISH! DODOS WITH NO BRAINS!' he whispered, as loud as he could whisper.

'If you want us to help you,' advised Hiccup, once they had reached the very cross Hero, and he carried on insulting them, 'perhaps you should be a little more polite.'

'*Some* help *you're* being!' whispered the upside-down-Hero-with-a-Healthy-Sense-of-Self-Respect. 'Those chains are my brilliant way of finding my way back! Only a genius like myself could think of such a thing! And you IDIOTS have just picked them all up!'

'Don't worry,' said Camicazi gaily. 'Stormfly here has an incredible sense of direction. She can find our way back in about five minutes.'

'And who are you, you blonde pipsqueak?'
Flashburn tried to draw his sword but of course all he
could do in that sticky web was wriggle around like a
caterpillar. 'And what are you doing in my territory?'

'I am not a blonde pipsqueak, I am a very
famous burglar and we're looking for the Lost Crown
of the Wilderwest,' said Camicazi, rather offended
but still chatty. (You should NEVER tell Camicazi
a secret. She was the chattiest person in the whole
Archipelago.) 'That horrible witch Excellinor sent us.
I think it's supposed to be in some sort of Fire Pit.
Have you seen it anywhere?'

'CURSE that double-crossing, triple-lying,
fork-tongued witch!' fumed Flashburn. 'Twenty
years ago that woman told my fortune before she
disappeared off the face of the earth... *I* would be
the King of the Wilderwest, she said, and of course
it seemed obvious, considering I'm the cleverest,
bravest, most charming, patient, good-natured, and
most brilliant swordfighter in the Archipelago! All I
had to do was find this beastly Crown and the thing
was a done deal...'

'So the witch has had you looking for this Crown
for the *last* twenty years?' gasped Hiccup.

This was exceptionally bad news.

'Well, obviously not *all the time*,' snapped Flashburn. 'What are you, some kind of gormless idiot? I have a school to run. But off and on, yes, I've been looking. And then she and her beastly son turn up in rags, after twenty years of not a word, not a line, and I put a roof over their heads, and gave her horrible son one-to-one swordfighting lessons...'

Aha, thought Hiccup. *So that's how the witch became the Castle Witch, and how Alvin got to be so good at swordfighting...*

'... and she got me to send away my forty Warriors on some ridiculous trumped-up Quest because she said they'd get in the way. And how does she repay me? She kidnaps me, just before you arrive, and tells me I have only three weeks to find the Crown or she'll leave me down here for ever!'

'You're lucky,' said Camicazi. 'She only gave US three hours...'

'She asked YOU to find the Crown? YOU?'

The Hero-with-a-Healthy-Sense-of-Self-Respect seemed to find this hilarious. 'A limping blonde pipsqueak, a freak-boy with a dragon on his head, and a skinny little weirdo? Oh that's ridiculous, that is...

'*I* am the greatest Hero the Archipelago has ever known!' spat Flashburn, which would have sounded more impressive if he hadn't been trapped upside-down in a Stickyworm web at the time. 'I am good-looking, I am brilliant, I am brave, I am intelligent...

'I have searched every tunnel, every inch of every cave, and if I haven't found the Crown or the Fire Pit after twenty years of looking, trust me, it isn't there to be found... Are you weird little freaks going to just stand there gawping, or are you going to cut me down?'

The Hero-with-a-Healthy-Sense-of-Self-Respect really needed to work on his manners. This did rather explain why he had so many enemies across the Archipelago.

'He's rude, isn't he?' said Fishlegs.

'Very rude,' said Camicazi. 'And he hasn't found the Crown, even after looking for twenty years,' she sneered. 'He doesn't seem to be the perfect Hero, after all.' Camicazi shook her head, enormously disappointed.

'That's because it's *impossible* to find the Crown,' hissed Flashburn furiously.

'Hiccup here is always doing impossible things,' said Camicazi, unimpressed, 'and he's half your size.'

'Shut up! Shut up!' Flashburn's upside-down face was so red he looked like he might explode. 'Shut up and hurry up! Release my brilliance to an admiring world... what are you waiting for?'

'That depends,' said Hiccup, slowly. 'Answer me a question first. If *you* were the King of the Wilderwest, would you free all the dragons and ban slavery in all its forms?'

Well, you can imagine, Flashburn laughed like a drain at that one. 'Of course I wouldn't. What a ridiculous question. Who would do all our dirty work if we didn't have dragons and slaves?'

Mmm.

'OK,' decided Hiccup. 'Cut him down but keep the chains round him. We can't risk this one making his way back to the swordfighting competition.'

So Camicazi cut him out of the web, and when he was the right way up he was an extremely cross man with a slightly sticky moustache. 'Untie me, you villains!' he panted. 'I give you my Hero's word I will not run away.'

But they had all read Flashburn's book,

Swordfighting with Style, which recommends many ways of outwitting your opponent, one of them being lying your head off.

'We're not in a trusting mood,' grinned Camicazi. 'And you're lucky Hiccup set you free at all, *I'd* have been tempted to leave you here.'

So off they set again, skating down the bewildering maze of tunnels for hour after hour, with the Hero skating behind them, on a long chain attached to Camicazi's wrist, complaining and whispering insults all the way.

'I told you,' hissed Flashburn. 'I have mapped every inch of these wretched tunnels, every winding corner is imprinted in my brilliant brain, and trust me, there is no Fire Pit— Hang on a second.'

The Hero cocked his head a trifle, mid-sentence, as if listening for something.

Click, click, click, and then, a very faint *rrrripping* noise.

Oh for Thor's sake.

RIPROARERS.

What could possibly have woken them up?

'Skate for your lives! Those creatures tear you apart!' shrieked Flashburn, in a dreadful whispering

Riproarers

~ STATISTICS ~

FEAR FACTOR: 8
ATTACK: 8
SPEED: 8
SIZE: 7
DISOBEDIENCE: 8

Riproarers are muscular cave-dwellers that, like their cousins the Raptortongues, can squeeze themselves into very tiny spaces. A swarm of Riproarers tears its victims to pieces.

bellow, eyes popping with terror…

… and Fishlegs put his head down on the ice and refused to move, limbs splayed like a sprawling starfish.

'Fishlegs!' whispered Hiccup tugging on his arm. 'Come on! You can do it, Fishlegs, you can do it! We have to get out of here NOW!'

But Fishlegs was exhausted from trying to keep up with everyone else. He wasn't a great skater at the best of times, but with Horrorcow attached to his shoulders it was impossible to balance and he had fallen over so many times he had had enough.

'No,' said Fishlegs, and he laid his head on the ice. 'I should never have come. I'm just holding you up. You can go on, if you want to. I'm just going to stay here and die.'

'The runt is right, we should just leave him,' hissed Flashburn, trying to skate but held up by Camicazi's chain. 'It's like I said down at the bottom of the cliff, he's not the stuff that Heroes are made of, he's just a jellyfish in a skirt. Do you not know what Riproarers do to you? I am a good-looking man, and the world needs me, I must be saved.'

Some Hero.

202

'Fishlegs, you really are going to die if you stay here,' hissed Hiccup.

'I don't care,' said Fishlegs, closing his eyes. 'I'm too tired. It's nice here. It's quiet. I'll just die here on this nice comfy ice. It's all hopeless anyway.'

Scritch, scritch, scritch, rip, rip.

Hiccup could hear the clicking of nails on the ice getting closer and closer and closer, as a pack of Riproarers came snuffling through the dark ice corridors towards them.

'Oh for Thor's sake... It's never hopeless, Fishlegs!' said Hiccup, desperately. 'We can still make it... Trust me, we can do this...'

I'm just going to lie here and die

11. RIPROARERS AND ELECTRICSTICKYS

In the desperation of the moment, an idea popped into Hiccup's mind.

Why hadn't the witch taken away the King's Things from him when she had the chance?

Because she knew he was going to need them down here…

He took the ticking-thing out of his pocket.

There were numerous arrows on the face of the ticking-thing. One told the time. Another predicted latitude. Another always pointed north.

And then there were various arrows that seemed to have no function at all, as far as Hiccup had been able to work out.

And there it was.

On one fat arrow that he had assumed was purely decorative, there was scratched a tiny little crown. A crown surrounded by tiny flames…

'Look! Fishlegs! The Crown!' panted Hiccup. 'Grimbeard's ticking-thing can show us the way to the Crown in the Fire Pit!'

Fishlegs opened a weary eye. Horrorcow relaxed her talons a second, and mooed approvingly.

'Luck is on our side, do you see, Fishlegs!'

A tiny dim light of hope arose within Fishlegs and he staggered to his feet. Somehow Hiccup and Camicazi supported him between them and carried on skating, dragging Flashburn, as the *scruffle scruffle* of feet came closer, and the panting grew louder.

DOWN the tunnels they slid, a shambolic crew indeed.

The Riproarers were gaining, gaining and beginning to howl as the four of them swerved round a corner. They entered a large cavern, and they were just skating through it when Toothless's sharp eyes spotted something, and he squeaked, 'L-l-l-look!'

Over to the right of the cave floor was a neat rectangular hole, cut into the floor by human hand, for nature could not cut those lines so straight.

'DOWN!' ordered

Hiccup, and one, two, three DOWN the hole jumped Fishlegs, Camicazi, Flashburn, and then last of all Hiccup, holding his rectangular shield above his head. Just as he leapt down the hole he had a stomach-melting sight of the first four Riproarers screaming round the corner, jaws a-gape before he slipped through the gap and...

CLANG!

The shield covered the hole completely.

It was as if the hole had been cut for the shield.

And maybe it HAD, *long, long ago...*

Hiccup hung from the straps, swinging. There was a three-foot drop to the floor.

'Let go!' Camicazi shouted up.

'No!' shouted Hiccup. 'They'll follow us!'

SCRITTCHHH! SCCRRITCH!

They heard the spine-curling jangle of knife-sharp claws landing on the metal of the shield above.

CLANG!

A great dent was punched into the shield as the full force of a Riproarer body landed on it, and the middle section of the metal was inches away from Hiccup's face...

Oh for Thor's sake...

SCRUFFLE SCRUFFLE SCRUFFLE as paws
and talons picked at the edge of the shield...

Any second now and they would get a good grip
and lift the entire shield out of the hole, Hiccup and
all...

One talon got right through under the shield and
heaved it upwards...

'CAMICAZI!' screamed Hiccup, as he
felt himself being pulled upwards. 'GRAB AN
ELECTRICSTICKY AND THROW IT AT THE
SHIELD!'

The shield lifted further, and Hiccup was staring
into the repellent face of the Riproarer, the stuff of
nightmares, black frothing slobber foaming at the
mouth, red-veined eyes quivering, its hot,
indescribably stinking and repellent breath scalding
Hiccup's cheeks.

'AAAARRRRGHHHHHHHH!' screamed
Hiccup as the final heave took him up into the gap and
the mouth opened for the bite...

... and in the very splinter of time...

SPLAT!

With a gorgeously squelchy squishing noise
the Electricsticky landed on the shield, stuck there
quivering, and the entire shield became electrified.
The Riproarer gave a horrified scream and jumped back
as if bitten simultaneously by a hive full of hornets.
The shield clanged back into place, Hiccup swinging
violently from the leather straps, as...

SPLAT! SPLAT!

Camicazi threw two more of the Electricstickys

on to the shield. She was wearing her burglary gloves, so they didn't give HER an electric shock, and of course Camicazi was expert at throwing pretty much anything. As Hiccup dropped to the ground she grinned from ear to ear for the first time since they had been in the dungeon.

'Genius!' she crowed. 'Now you really *are* a genius, Hiccup! You see… we're going to do it! It's a sign from fate that we're going to make it…'

'Don't count your chickens…' panted Hiccup, thoroughly rattled from his close-up with the Riproarer. Camicazi hadn't looked into its mad staring eyes, and seen how close they had been to being torn to pieces. 'And don't forget that if we want to see daylight again, we have to go back up there and face them. They'll wait for us… Trust me, they'll wait for us…'

'But the blonde pipsqueak is right,' panted Flashburn. 'This is extraordinary. Twenty years I've searched these tunnels, and I've never seen that hole before. This is a part of the maze that I've never been down.'

'That was TOOTHLESS who saw that!' crowed Toothless.

'Yes, Toothless, you're very, very clever,' said

Hiccup. 'Look!' he exclaimed, excitedly pointing to the other side of the cave.

The broken ticking-thing was going a little crazy. It gave twenty-five frantic ticks in a row, played the Hooligan National Anthem backwards, and then popped a spring and fell silent, poor thing.

There, in that dead darkness, there was a golden glow of flickering life.

A bright circle in the cave floor which, as they approached nearer, was a golden mine, a pit of flames that licked the black walls in glorious, leaping rivers of fire.

'I don't believe it…' gasped Flashburn, eyes goggling with amazement. 'I DO NOT believe it! Twenty years of my brilliance and bravery, searching every inch of this dungeon at terrible risk to my precious person, and you ridiculous freak-children have found the Fire Pit. How can this be possible? This must be an accident!'

'There are no accidents,' advised Fishlegs, kindly.

That was a supernatural sight.

Right in the heart of the mountain, in the centre of the icy maze of tunnels, was the Fire Pit.

Earth, water, stone and fire.

THE FIRE PIT.

All four elements guarding the precious Lost Crown of the Wilderwest.

Just at that glorious triumphant moment, echoing down the tunnels, a wicked whisper came.

It was the same sound that Hiccup had heard earlier on the Angry Face of Angry Mountain, but it was louder now.

The words were in Dragonese, hissed in a furious, bitter tone, truly terrifying in its savagery. But if it had been scary out in the open, how much scarier still was it in the darkness, echoing hollowly down the tunnels. Enough to turn the spine to water it was, and send each hair shivering upwards to attention.

'MAKE RED your claws with HUMAN BLOOD... OBLITERATE the HUMAN FILTH.. Torch the humans like a WOOD The REBELLion is coMiNG...'

'What is *that*?' asked Flashburn the Hero.

'It's nothing… Nothing at all… It's just trying
to scare us…' said Hiccup, frantically stroking
Horrorcow's back.

'And it's succeeding,' gasped Fishlegs.

'Ignore it,' whispered Hiccup. 'It may sound
close, but trust me, it's still miles away. It won't be able
to get through the electrified shield.'

Hiccup took off his rucksack.

All three of their fire-suits had a
few holes in them, what with one
thing and another. 'Camicazi
could you lend me a fire-
glove?' said Hiccup. 'And has
anyone got a foot piece that
hasn't got holes in it?'

Between the three of
them, they could put together
a reasonably-complete fire-
suit, and Hiccup put it on,
turning as he wriggled

the helmet-and-mask bit over his head, so that the other two wouldn't see his forehead.

'Now hang on a minute, you little freaks.' Poor Flashburn was practically crying now. '*I'm* the Hero here, and I've been looking for this Fire Pit for twenty years… It's *my* Impossible Quest… Surely you can't let the skinny weirdo go in instead of ME.'

Wordlessly, Camicazi wound one chain off Flashburn, tied one end around a large stalagmite and dangled the other down into the Fire Pit.

'It'll do,' said Camicazi, checking Hiccup all over for holes.

Hiccup took hold of the chain.

Climbing into fire is always scary, even when you are wearing a fire-suit.

He took a deep breath and thought of his father.

Nobody said being a Hero was going to be easy.

He climbed down into the pit of fire.

There *were* a few holes in that fire-suit after all.

As he climbed down, Hiccup could feel the burning through the holes, as if he were being pressed by hot coins on his thigh, on his arm, on the back of his calf.

Inside the pit, he walked through the flames to find himself standing in the middle of a circle of fire, in a cave that no human had visited for at least one hundred years.

And there, in the middle of the cavern, lay the golden Crown of the Wilderwest.

Sitting there, quiet as you please, minding its own business, with no idea that it had caused Flashburn so much trouble, as if it had been waiting for Hiccup all this time.

The Crown was dazzlingly beautiful, a perfect circle of shining gold.

Hiccup reached out a shaking hand to take it.

And he froze like he had been stung, and just stopped himself from crying out.

For curled up inside the Crown itself, the same colour as the rock, was a small, brown dragon.

Curled up inside the Crown itself was a small, brown dragon.

Oh that Grimbeard the Ghastly!

Of course there had to be some trick, some trap! And now he came to think of it, of course there had to be a dragon. The fire was burning off a black substance.* But something must have set that black substance on fire, and that something was, of course, a dragon.

He didn't recognize the species, but he would have bet his whole life on the guess that it was something deadly poisonous.

There was nothing for it, though. He would have to take the Crown without waking the dragon.

All of his burglary skills would come in handy, now.

Shaking slightly, he drew his sword.

Holding his breath, he carefully, carefully, slowly, slowly, reached and touched the Crown.

The dragon lay, still as stone.

Hiccup took a very delicate hold of the Crown, and gently pulled.

And pulled.

The Crown did not budge.

But the dragon lifted its head and opened its eyes.

---

*This could have been peat or coal.

12. THE LOST KINGDOM OF THE WILDERWEST

He was a very ancient dragon indeed. Dried up and brown, like an old prune, barely able to open his eyes, wrinkles so deep and folded he was like a crumpled map.

Hiccup had never seen such an old dragon.

For a split second, Hiccup was convinced the dragon was going to kill him. He had brought back his head like dragons do, like a rattlesnake about to strike.

And Hiccup tried to move his sword, but it was as if his arm were turned to stone.

Dragon-eye met boy-eye, the golden cat's eye meeting Hiccup's blue, there in the middle of that circle of fire.

Hiccup's head began to spin. He closed his eyes.

'Who are you?' asked the dragon – but he already knew the answer.

'I am Hiccup Horrendous Haddock the Third. And I want to take this Crown, please,' said Hiccup politely. 'Who are you?'

'Well, Hiccup the Third, I am the Wodensfang and I am supposed to kill whoever tries to take this Crown...' His voice was a barely-there hiss, the faraway whisper of a skeletonleaf.

'Please don't,' said Hiccup, still with his eyes closed.

There was a long silence.

'Because humans and dragons cannot live together,' said the dragon.

'You sound like the Dragon Furious,' said Hiccup, opening his eyes. 'I don't believe that that is true.'

'Once I believed as you did,' said the dragon very, very wearily, 'but I have changed my mind.'

'Of course they can live together!' said Hiccup fiercely. 'Some of my best friends are dragons! It's just that things have gone wrong somehow...

'The dragons have become enslaved, when they ought to be free. But you HAVE to believe that people and dragons can be better. You HAVE to believe in a better world...'

'And is this what you would do, Hiccup the Third, if *you* were the King of the Wilderwest? You would free all the dragons?' asked the ancient dragon. 'You would work to make sure that humans and dragons live together in peace?'

Hiccup did not want to be the King of the Wilderwest.

But sometimes we all have to grow up.

'Yes,' said Hiccup. 'I promise.'

The dragon sighed again.

'The problem is,' said the dragon, 'I am an old, old dragon, and you are not the first to make me that promise. And history has a way of repeating itself.'

The Wodensfang

'Maybe it doesn't have to,' said Hiccup.

'Hear my story,' said the dragon, 'and perhaps you will change your mind...'

'I'm in a bit of a hurry,' said Hiccup.

The Wodensfang looked at him with his hypnotic eyes.

There was a distinct edge to his ancient voice.

'We have all the time in the world,' said the Wodensfang.

'We have all the time in the world,' repeated Hiccup.

Hiccup sat down cross-legged, laid his sword on his knees and listened to the story, inside the circle of fire, in the icy heart of Angry Mountain.

'You see,' said the Wodensfang, 'you are not the first human to have the name of Hiccup. You are not the first human to carry that sword.'

Oh dear. Oh dear. Hiccup was getting that black-beetles-on-his-scalp feeling again.

'The first human who made me that promise was called... Hiccup Horrendous Haddock the First...'

THE STORY OF HICCUP HORRENDOUS HADDOCK THE FIRST

'Five or six centuries ago,' said the dragon, 'when I was young, it was a very Dark Age, and the dragons and humans were at war. The leader of the dragon army, a great Sea Dragon known as Merciless, had looked into the future and seen that he would be killed by a human by the name of Hiccup.

'He had learnt that a human of this name was living on an island in the Archipelago, and I was sent on a mission to kill all humans on this one particular island.

'Unfortunately, I flew so low over the little island that I became caught in the branches of a tree. I hung there for two days, terribly wounded in my chest, and tangling myself round and round like a fish on a line, growing weaker and weaker.

'I was rescued by a small boy, about nine years old.

'Ironically, he was the very same boy I had been sent there to kill... The boy called Hiccup the First.

'Hiccup the First climbed the tree where I was captured, and untangled me. You have to realize, that was an extraordinary act of bravery, for in those days, dragons and humans were mortal enemies. I had never even SEEN a human up close before. Just killed them from a distance. I could have incinerated the child with one single breath of flame, taken him out with one slash of my dying talons.

'But the boy freed me, and then he nursed me back to health. With his clever human fingers, he sewed up the wound in my chest, put on herbs that healed it. Look, you can see the scar even now!'

Hiccup looked. There it was. A scar over his wrinkled brown heart. A faint line, the tiny jagged marks of sewing hundreds of years old. A boy's sewing, uneven and crooked.

A scar in the exact same place that Toothless had a scar.

And the Dragon Furious had a scar.

Three dragons, each with a scar above their heart.

Three boys, all called Hiccup.

'Once I was well again, I flew away, back to the north. But I kept returning. I taught the boy our language, Dragonese. He, in turn, taught me to understand Norse. Hiccup was the first human to ride upon a dragon's back. My back. And the more I got to know this Hiccup, the more I saw something special in the human race that we dragons did not have. Love. Imagination. Creativity. Communication through language. Foresight. All of these things the humans could teach us, if we allowed them to survive. But the humans had not yet developed modern weapons of war, and the dragons were hunting them to extinction...

'I had a dream. A foolish dream, a hope that perhaps human beings and dragons could co-exist in the world.

'So I resolved to save the humans from destruction.

'Now, there was a certain jewel that Merciless was guarding. The Dragon Jewel was the only thing that Merciless was afraid of, a jewel in the form of a

piece of amber that
had the power to
destroy dragons
utterly and for ever.
The jewel was hidden,
long ago, inside the secret
compartment of a sword.'

Hiccup gave a gasp.

'You are right,' said the dragon. 'It was the
very sword that you have right in front of you. The
Dragonsword. The sword was guarded by a terrible
dragon in a Fire Pit, a far more terrible dragon than
I am.'

Hiccup gasped again.

'You are right again,' said the dragon. 'It was
the very Fire Pit that we are sitting in right now.
History, you see, has a way of repeating itself.

'Long ago, I stole the Dragonsword from the
Fire Pit.

'I gave it to Hiccup the First. I showed
him the jewel hidden within.

'I gave this jewel, terrible as it was,
into the hands of a human.

'Tell me, was I right to trust a human

226

in this way? Or was I betraying my own kind? You see the boy promised me. He promised me that he would not use this gift for evil. He promised that he would make sure that dragons and humans lived in harmony.'

'I don't know whether you were right,' whispered Hiccup, white as coral. 'I really don't know... What happened next?'

'Well, when Merciless flew to assassinate Hiccup the First, the boy stood, barefoot and defenceless in rags, outside his grass-topped hut and held up the jewel. The great dragon was young, but he was as large as a flying mountain. His wing-tips were so wide that they seemed to stretch to either horizon. There was such a fire within that dragon it could have turned the whole island into

The Dragon Jewel was once hidden inside the secret compartment of a SWORD...

dust and ashes with one single exhalation.

'But the amber, so small that it could fit hidden within one man's fist, that one tiny jewel made the mighty carnivore hold his breath.

'It was the one thing he was afraid of...

'Hiccup the First made the mighty Merciless promise to call off the Red-Rage. He ordered him to disband the Dragon Army, and to live again a loner.

'"You must never return to the Archipelago," said Hiccup the First, "or the fate that fortune foretold will overcome you."

'So that was the end of the Red-Rage in those times. Merciless flew to the north, and to the Open Sea. He lived so long a loner, that perhaps over the centuries he forgot his youth as leader of a dragon army, and became quite an ordinary killer. Rumour was that several hundred years later, he was known only as "the Green Death", one of the many monsters that terrorize the Deep Sea. Did you say something?'

'*I killed him*,' whispered Hiccup Horrendous Haddock the Third. 'He returned to the Archipelago and I killed the Green Death...'*

The Wodensfang gave a dry laugh. 'Yes, that's

---

*See *How to Train Your Dragon*, the first volume of Hiccup's memoirs.

right, he was killed by a Hiccup in the end after all...'

Isn't fate artistic?

'Meanwhile, Hiccup the First decided to use the Dragon Jewel further. "I will use the jewel," said the boy, "for a very particular purpose."

'He began to train more dragons. He trained them to farm, to hunt, to herd sheep and deer. He taught others on the islands all around to do the same, and with the dragons' help they could manage the deer herds twice as well as they could before. And they grew twice as fat, twice as strong.

'It worked for the dragons too. The boy did not treat the dragons as the dragons are treated now. They were equals. They sat around the fire as equal partners. They were fed first at the hunt. The boy asked their opinion before attacks, and talked with them as naturally as if they were human beings.

'The boy set up a new kingdom, a kingdom of peace and equality, in which all were equal, and where dragons and humans worked together for the common good. And that was nearly the end of the story.'

NEARLY THE END

'You see!' said Hiccup. 'The boy kept his promise!'

The Wodensfang sighed. 'He kept his promise while he lived. But we forgot how short human life is. To us dragons, a human life is as short as a butterfly's. The boy never betrayed me in life. But he could not keep his promise beyond his death.'

Quietness in the Fire Pit.

'The boy's descendants were not as trustworthy as the boy was. They used the power I had given them over the dragons for evil. They enslaved the dragons. The humans got worse and worse until they ended in...'

'Grimbeard the Ghastly,' said Hiccup.

'Grimbeard the Ghastly,' repeated the Wodensfang. 'And you know how that story ended. So when Grimbeard came to me at the end of his dreadful life, a great hairy ruin, with a wild look in his eye, to ask me to guard the Crown of the Wilderwest so that no human should ever have the power that he had again, of course I agreed. Why should I permit YOU to take the Crown? Why should I make the same mistake TWICE?'

Hiccup did not answer. It was a good question.

The boy and the dragon sat looking down at the Crown. It was a big responsibility, that circle of gold.

The boy was thinking:

There have been two Hiccups before me, both far greater human beings than I am, who have tried to civilize this godforsaken part of the world, and they have failed, as completely as if they had never lived. Why should I even TRY *to do something that is doomed to failure right from the start?*

The dragon was thinking much the same.

Hiccup looked at the perfectly ordinary sword, sitting on his knees.

After a while Hiccup said, 'When I first found this sword, by accident, I did not know its name was the Dragonsword. So I took it to my grandfather, Old Wrinkly, and asked him to name it for me.

'Old Wrinkly named it "Endeavour". He said that the name was important, because "to endeavour" means trying to do something even when you know you might be beaten before you even start.'

The old dragon lifted his eyes up to the boy's face.

'And then he said something that I have never forgotten, though it seemed a little strange to me at the time. He said:

'"History is a set of repeating circles, like the tides. The wind *does* blow through the ruins of Tomorrow. But it is more a question of two steps forward, one step back. Humans and dragons make the same mistakes, again and again, but things do get better over time."

'Maybe...' and now Hiccup was struggling to find the right grown-up words. 'Maybe... forgotten Heroes like the first two Hiccups have made the world just a little better than it would have been if they had never lived?'

The Wodensfang finished the sentence. 'And perhaps your grandfather was right. Over time, over thousands and thousands of years, those little betters become a large and greater good.'

There was a long, long pause.

'So if I let you take this Crown, will you promise that you will use it to make sure that humans and dragons live together in peace? Will you promise that you won't let the Crown fall into the wrong hands?' asked the Wodensfang.

The wrong hands were out there, waiting: the witch, and Alvin, and Flashburn.

Hiccup tried not to think of all the things he was going to have to do in order to become the King.

He was going to have to get them all out of here alive.

He was going to have to vanquish the witch at the well.

He was going to have to defeat everybody else in the swordfighting competition.

Then he would have to persuade everyone to free all the dragons, and he knew how well *that* was going to go down.

It was the Impossible Task to end all Impossible Tasks.

'I promise to try my hardest,' said Hiccup.

'In which case,' said the dragon, 'maybe that's good enough for me. Take the Crown, and live.'

'Thank you,' said Hiccup, picking up the Crown to put it in his waistcoat.

As he picked up the Crown, the walls of the Fire Pit seemed to explode with sound.

A terrible scream from the same voice he had heard earlier, but now it was shrieking so loud, that his eardrums reverberated and the very flames seemed to flicker with the noise.

'HUNt Them, EVerybody!
There's four of them in
here, human SCUM!'

'He's got it! He's got it! After him, all! The
wretched little human boy has got the Crown!
Riproarers! Slitherfangs! Breathquenchers! ALL!
Hunt him down, creatures of this darkness, hunt him
down!'

For Thor's sake, thought Hiccup, his hands over
his ears, *that sounds just like the Dragon Furious... But
how is that possible? He's far too large to get down that
well...*

The Wodensfang was quite unaffected by the
noise. Maybe he was too old to be scared.

'There is another entrance to the dungeons,'
explained the Wodensfang, responding as if he could
read Hiccup's mind. 'A great cave in the Gorge of

the Thunderbolt of Thor. A cave perfectly large
enough to admit a Sea Dragon, even of the size of
the Dragon Furious.'

Quickly, but very carefully, Hiccup picked up
the ancient dragon. He was once fat, but now he was
lighter than air, poor old thing, like a little bony leaf,
or a scratchy scarab beetle, all bones and skin. Hiccup
put him in his waistcoat with the crown.

'OK,' said Hiccup, 'we've got to get out of
here...'

'My, my,' said the Wodensfang admiringly,
blinking up at him like a little brown papoose. 'I'd
forgotten the blind optimism of youth. What a very
great pleasure to meet it again, after so many years.'

'No problemo,' said Hiccup reassuringly. 'We can
do this.'

Easier.
Said.
Than.
Done.

13. GET YOUR SKATES ON!!!!

Out of the Fire Pit Hiccup climbed. He had never climbed so fast before.

Camicazi hauled him up the last bit. Fishlegs put out a small fire that had started on his back. They were white and shaking, petrified by that appalling noise.

Even in the horror of the moment, Toothless noticed the brown dragon in HIS place in Hiccup's waistcoat.

'Who's that in T-t-toothless's place?' he hissed furiously.

'NEVER MIND THAT NOW! GET YOUR SKATES ON!' yelled Hiccup. 'WE NEED TO GET BACK UP THERE BEFORE THEY START THE SWORDFIGHTING COMPETITION! STORMFLY, LEAD THE WAY!'

'BUT YOU'VE WOKEN UP ALL THE CAVE DRAGONS, YOU FREAK IGNORAMUSES!' shrieked Flashburn, hopping from foot to foot in terrified fury, still whispering, as if that would make any difference when there was the most horrific cacophony going on. 'THERE'S A REASON WHY

I ONLY EVER SEARCH THESE CAVES IN THE
WINTER! LISTEN TO THAT NOISE! WE'RE
GOING TO BE ANNIHILATED!'

The noise was truly ear-splitting, like four
hundred Furies screaming all at once.

'He's got it! He's got it! After him, all!
The wretched little human boy hAs
got the Crown! Riproarers!
BreathQuenchers! Brainpickers!
ALL! HUNT HIM DOWN, Creatures
of this darkness, HUNT HIM
DOWN!!!'

screamed the voice of the Red-Rage in a ghastly echo
that trembled down the tunnels and echoed back to
itself.

And the voice was answered by the most spine-
chilling, blood-curdling howling of Riproarers and

Breathquenchers and Thor knows what else, as every dragon in the entire cave tunnelwarren appeared to be waking up.

'We have no choice,' said Hiccup grimly. 'And we'll be all right. Something will turn up. Draw your swords everybody.'

'Something will turn up?' shrieked the enraged Flashburn. '*Something will turn up?* What do you mean, something will turn up? Why are you listening to this bozo? OW!'

This was as he was practically yanked off his feet by Camicazi, who had already set off and was pulling on his chain.

They skated like fury through the tunnels, through the darkness. There were no sign of any dragons yet, they must all have been up on the other side of the electrified shield.

'Have… you… got… the… Crown?' panted Fishlegs.

'Yup,' said Hiccup, pointing to his waistcoat.

'I don't believe it,' gasped Flashburn, and the only word for how he felt at that moment is a word in Dragonese, and the word is BOGGLE-SMASHED. 'Twenty years of looking… *twenty years*… and the

Crown is found
by a couple of weirdos
and a limping pipsqueak!'

'THIS LIMPING PIPSQUEAK IS SKATING
FASTER THAN YOU ARE!' yelled Camicazi, 'KEEP
UP, WHY DON'T YOU?'

Back they skated to the tunnel where the
Electricstickys still clung, glowing, to Hiccup's Roman
shield.

Above the shield were the most horrific noises of
howling, and scuffling, and talons being sharpened.

'Push up the shield with your sword, Camicazi,'
said Hiccup.

'What in Thor's name are you doing?' panted
Flashburn. 'They're up there! They're all up there!'

'Do it, Camicazi!' said Hiccup.

And then Hiccup gave a shriek of his own, at
the top of his voice, in Dragonese:

'Aaaaaghhhh! WE'RE BEING ATTACKED
BY BRAINPICKERS!'

There was a sudden, uneasy silence from above
the shield.

Camicazi poked the shield with her sword and it
lifted up as easily as a trapdoor.

A Riproarer thrust its revolting head tentatively
through the opening, weird taloned whiskers
quivering.

Hiccup pointed at Fishlegs, standing there with
Horrorcow attached to his head.

'AAAAGHHHH!' shrieked Hiccup.
'BRAINPICKERS!!!'

'AAAAAAGHHH!' shrieked the Riproarer,
abruptly disappearing. 'BRAINPICKERS!!!'

'BRAINPICKERS!' 'BRAINPICKERS!'
'BRAINPICKERS!!!'

The tunnel above erupted with the sound of panicking dragons, screaming and running away. Everything, you see, is frightened of *something*, and Brainpickers are one of the most feared dragons in the Archipelago, because nobody likes the idea of having their brains sucked out through their ears.

A couple more dragons poked their heads through, took one look at Fishlegs, shrieked, and disappeared again.

Fishlegs twigged what was going on, climbed up and thrust his entire head, with Horrorcow attached, through the trapdoor. There was a final stampede in the tunnel above, dragons screaming, trampling over each other, forked tails disappearing into the darkness... and then silence.

'They've gone,' Fishlegs announced.

'They've *gone*????' gasped a flabbergasted Flashburn. 'What do you mean, *they've gone*?'

Hiccup climbed up after Fishlegs, and Camicazi tore the Electricksticks from the shield with her gloved hands, and handed the shield wordlessly to Hiccup, before scrambling up herself, and giving Flashburn a couple of strong yanks on the chain.

'Are you coming, Flashy boy, or are you just

242

going to stand there with your mouth open?'
demanded Camicazi. 'We've got to be quick, before
those dragons realize it's a trick.'

They had to help him up because his arms were
still tied.

Through the tunnels those young Vikings fled.
There were no sign of any dragons, and the Dragon
Furious's rage seemed to have quietened now that they
were higher up the tunnel warren.

They rounded the final corner. There was the
cauldron, lying on one side.

'What... are you going to do about the witch...'
panted Fishlegs as they came to a screeching halt
beside it.

'I'll think of something,' said Hiccup, and he and
Fishlegs and Camicazi all got into the cauldron.

'You mean,' shrieked Flashburn, 'the witch is still
UP there?'

'That's right,' said Hiccup. 'All we have to do is
defeat the witch, and then we're home free. Get in.'

But Flashburn refused.

He had spent the last three weeks in the
darkness, eating little cave dragons raw, which is
depressing for starters. Then he had resigned himself

to death at the ghastly maw of a Stickyworm, which would have been a yucky way to go, but at least there would have been a kind of glory to it, a Hero dying in the course of his Quest and all that sort of thing.

But then these little weirdos had turned up.

For Flashburn's entire life he had been the one making the clever remarks, showing off, leading from the front. Now here he was, sticky all over, wrapped in chains, looking perfectly ridiculous.

Flashburn had never failed at anything before. Sure, the Quest for the Crown had been frustrating, but he had consoled himself with the thought that it was impossible, and, again, there was a kind of glory to endlessly pursuing an impossible quest.

But now, in less than two hours, the little weirdos had found the Fire Pit he had been seeking for twenty years, taken the Crown, defeated the terrifying cave dragons he and his warriors had been avoiding all this time, and now they were proposing to face that horrible witch and her horrible fingernails.

Even the truly odd-looking one with the dragon on his head seemed to be some kind of super-hero with the power to terrify dragons just by looking at them.

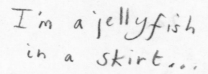

I'm a jellyfish in a skirt...

Flashburn's ego had fallen. The Hero had lost his mojo. And when an ego the size of Flashburn's starts falling, it has a long way to go.

He lay down on the cave floor beside the cauldron. 'No,' said Flashburn. 'I won't get in.'

'Oh, come on,' cajoled Camicazi. 'Remember what you said at the cliff. Are you the stuff that Heroes are made of? Or are you a jellyfish in a skirt?'

'I'm a jellyfish,' said Flashburn.

'I can't face that witch. You leave me here and go on up without me.'

Hiccup looked at Camicazi and Fishlegs.

'I'll deal with this on my own, and you can come up after I've defeated the witch,' said Hiccup. 'She'll only be strong enough to pull one of us up at a time anyway.'

'Toothless'll come with you,' said Toothless, bristling with jealousy, 'even though s-s-someone else is in Toothless's place... because TOOTHLESS is Hiccup's dragon... Hiccup's very s-s-special dragon... Hiccup needs Toothless to help him.'

Camicazi and Fishlegs got out.

'We can't leave you here,' Camicazi explained to Flashburn, 'because you may be a jellyfish in a skirt, but you're OUR jellyfish, and that's the way things work with us.'

Camicazi began to unwrap him from his chains.

'PULL ME UP!'

Hiccup shouted up the well.

The face of the witch appeared far away, a tiny circle of light at the top.

'Throw... up... the... Crown... first...' the answer came echoing back.

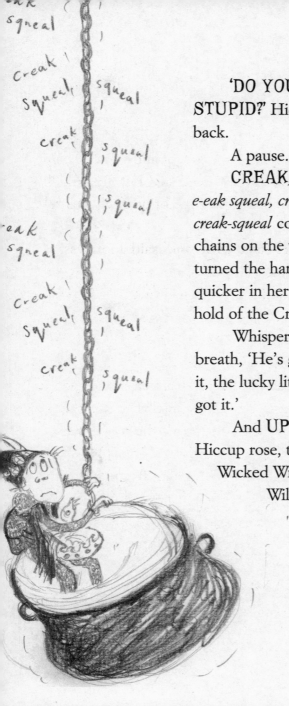

'DO YOU THINK I'M STUPID?' Hiccup called back.

A pause.

CREAK, *squeal, cre-e-eak squeal, creak-squeal, creak-squeal* complained the chains on the well as the witch turned the handle quicker and quicker in her greed to get hold of the Crown.

Whispering under her breath, 'He's got it, he's got it, the lucky little rat has got it.'

And UP, UP, UP Hiccup rose, to face the Wicked Witch of the Wilderwest.

THINGS ARE GOING WELL...

Hiccup now has **NINE** *of the King's Lost Things.*

*These are the Things that Grimbeard the Ghastly scattered
and hid across the Archipelago, so that only a Hero of
truly extraordinary ability could gather them together, and
become the next King of the Wilderwest.*

Surely this means that HICCUP is that Hero?

Read on, dear reader, and we shall see...

14. THE WICKED WITCH OF THE WILDERWEST

'Ooh dear, she looks nasty,' whispered the Wodensfang as they came out of the darkness and into the light and the cauldron hit the top of the well with a CLUNK.

'Give me the Crown…' hissed the witch, eyes a-gleam, fingers pointing warningly towards Hiccup like knives. She was a sight to make a man faint, she was, faint with fear on the spot.

Toothless was so terrified that he forgot he was

supposed to be being helpful.

He tried to do his normal dive down the front of Hiccup's waistcoat, remembered at the last minute that it was currently occupied by the Wodensfang, so lifted up Hiccup's helmet instead, and crawled under there to hide.

'Give me my father, first,' said Hiccup Horrendous Haddock the Third.

The witch smiled, and *what* a nasty smile it was.

She twirled her fingernails, each pointed nail gleaming with death.

'Now, Hiccup,' cooed the witch, 'you are an intelligent boy. You know that it isn't wise to trust the word of a Treacherous. The clue is in the name, really. You will give me that Crown, and you will hand over the King's Things, or else I shall scratch you to death,' grinned the witch. 'For it is better for you to be a live Nothing, than a dead Hero.'

'In which case,' said Hiccup Horrendous Haddock the Third, walking towards the cupboard, 'I choose not to give you anything at all, for I am not afraid of you.'

'You should be!' shrieked the witch, 'You should be!'

The witch wrestled him for a second, hand-to-hand, so that

Hiccup's palms were dyed purple with the poison. And then she scratched him as he walked, and the fingernails pierced the fire-suit.

Hiccup carried on walking.

She pierced him again.

Nothing.

Hiccup carried on walking.

Again and again she scratched him, raked him with those poisoned talons, scraping deep into his skin, dripping poison on his hands, but still he walked, calmly towards the cupboard.

This had never happened to the witch before.

First, she was bewildered, and then she became scared herself.

'*Who* ARE *you*?' she asked querulously. 'Why are you not scared?' she screeched, suddenly small and frightened. 'You know that these fingernails are poisoned with the most deadly poison known to man. Death is scary. How can you not be scared of Death itself?'

Hiccup smiled. He looked the witch in the eyes.

'I am not scared because *I* know something that *you* do not know. The most deadly poison known to man is Vorpent poison, and I am immune to the poison of the Venomous Vorpent. Ask your son to tell you the story. It was all his fault, really.'

The witch screamed as if someone had thrown a bucket of boiling water over her. One second she was this swooping, vengeful Fury. The next she crumpled in on herself, like a collapsing deck of cards.

Hiccup carried on walking to the cupboard.

He took out the key-that-opens-all-locks with trembling hands.

Please, Thor, let him be in here... He **MUST** *be in here, for the key is one of the King's Things and I haven't used it yet...*

Hiccup opened the door with the key.

There in the cupboard were the two heads of Stoick the Vast and UG the Uglithug...

For one dreadful moment, Hiccup thought that was all there was, for he had heard a horrible fairytale once about a witch who kept heads in cupboards...

... but thankfully the heads were attached to the rest of their bodies.

THANK THOR AND FREYA AND WODEN AND EVERYONE ELSE!

Giddy with relief, Hiccup cut the ropes and gags that bound Stoick and UG and they staggered out of the cupboard.

'Father!' cried Hiccup, and 'Hiccup!' cried Stoick, and it is difficult to know who was happier, as they enveloped each other in a joyful embrace.

UG staggered out of that cupboard like a deflated balloon.

He had had a particularly dreadful time with the witch, who had kept on taking him out of the cupboard and beating him at chess, before putting him back in again, and saying she might kill him tomorrow. The experience had been a humbling one.*

'Hop in,' said Hiccup genially to the witch, pointing his sword Endeavour at her, and opening wide the cupboard door.

Well, what could the witch do?

---

* The witch may have wanted to pay UG back for imprisoning her for twenty years in a tree trunk. Please see *How to Break a Dragon's Heart*.

Her venom had no bite any more. She was like a rattle snake with no rattle. A puff adder with no puff. A Hero with no mojo.

Her scary fingernails drooped.

'Quick! Quick!' said Hiccup.

The witch got in the cupboard.

Hiccup reached out with the Sword Endeavour, and cut the key from around her neck.

He locked the door of the cupboard twice, with both keys, just to make sure.

'By the way,' he shouted through the keyhole. 'You're very good at the "wicked" stuff, but you're terrible at chess.'

He walked to the chess table and moved a pawn one space.

'Checkmate,' said Hiccup Horrendous Haddock the Third.

Stoick and UG the Uglithug stared at him open-mouthed.

'We've got to get the others up now,' said Hiccup briskly. 'Get that handle moving. Quick! Quick!'

With the bulging muscles of Stoick the Vast and UG the Uglithug working the handle, well, that cauldron came up licketty-split, even with Fishlegs,

Camicazi and Flashburn sitting in it.

Toothless's little snout came peeping out from under Hiccup's helmet.

'H-h-has she gone??' he said warily.

'She's in the cupboard,' replied Hiccup, carefully removing him from under the helmet, and Toothless puffed out his little chest and flew over to show off in front of Stormfly, and shout insults through the keyhole.

Stormfly wasn't concentrating, she was too busy wolfing down fortune cookies. And everyone else joined in, for they realized they had missed breakfast, and skating down ice tunnels being chased by Riproarers and who-knows-what is hungry work.

Hiccup listened down the well.

All was eerily quiet down there, so quiet that if it were not for the fact that Hiccup's eardrums were still ringing from the sound, it could almost be that the whole Red-Rage incident had all been just a nightmare.

What had happened to the Dragon Furious?

Had he turned back because the tunnels got too small for him? Would he make his way back to the Gorge of the Thunderbolt of Thor and then return, with a dreadful army, many times larger than the one that Hiccup had defeated at the cliff-top?

The smashed ticking-thing had begun to tick again, a little erratically, tick-TOCK, tick-TOCK...

It reminded Hiccup that time was running out.

'Right,' said Hiccup, 'now we're going to have to hurry if we're going to be in time for the swordfighting competition...'

But it was all too much for Flashburn, the Hero who had lost his Mojo.

'RUN FOR YOUR L-I-I-I-IVES!' shouted Flashburn and he shot out the door.

UG the Uglithug hopped from foot to foot.

He had a squashed cigar clamped between his teeth.

The witch had drawn *his* venom too, and seeing one of the greatest Heroes in the Archipelago running from the room was enough to tip him over the edge.

Without saying a thing, he followed Flashburn.

15. THINGS GO SURPRISINGLY WELL IN THE SWORDFIGHTING COMPETITION

Outside in the Battle Arena, the competition could wait no longer.

The Eldest Elder had already read out the competitors for the first heats, and the rules. The winner of each swordfight would go on to fight another winner, and so on, until eventually there were only two competitors left.

The aim of the swordfight was to disarm rather than maim or kill the opponent (although accidents do, of course, happen).

The Tribes were getting restless, and beginning to sit down cross-legged and sing, 'Why are we wa-a-a-a-iting...'

The Eldest Elder was getting jumpy.

They were already three minutes late, and although that witch seemed to have disappeared, thank Thor, she might pop out at any moment like a malevolent jack-in-a-box and start complaining.

'I'm afraid,' said the Eldest Elder at last, 'we can

258

wait no longer, we shall have to start the competition. It is a sad day for all of us, and I am sorry for the Hooligans, for they shall have neither their Chief, nor their Stand-in-Chief to fight for them, but rules are rules I'm afraid, and promises are promises...

O HEAR YE, HEAR YE, HEAR YE! THE SWORDFIGHTING COMPETITION TO FIND THE NEXT KING OF THE WILDERWEST IS ABOUT TO BEGIN! BUGLER! SOUND THE BUGLE!'

The bugler was ju-u-u-ust putting the bugle to his lips to signal the start of the competition, when...

BANG!

The door of the fortune-telling hut flew open, and out ran a grimy, sticky, Flashburn, running at full tilt through the door.

BANG!

Closely followed by UG the Uglithug, though at not quite the pace of the Hero-with-a-Healthy-Sense-of-Self-Respect, because he had a belly as big as a battleship, and a considerable cigar habit, but still at an impressive lick for one of his circumference.

'Why bless my soul! Could that be... Flashburn! And UG!' cried the Eldest Elder, in astonishment.

'What were you doing in there and where have you—'

But neither the Hero nor the Uglithug Chieftain slowed their pace for one second, they just ran straight past the Eldest Elder, across the Battle Arena, past the eyes of a wondering eighteen Tribes and right towards the Great Entrance to the Castle.

'OPEN THE D-D-D-D-O-O-O-O-ORRRR!!!!!' yelled Flashburn the Hero, and the astonished sentries hurriedly opened the Great Doors, and out the Hero ran, without stopping, followed by the Mainland Chieftain.

The Tribesmen watched them go, open-mouthed, running down the Easy Way of Angry Mountain as fast as they could run. (And somersault, actually, because you can't run far down the Easy Way without it turning into a somersault.)

So that was the end of those two villains' ambitions, all their dreams, roly-polying their way out of the competition, and out of the story entirely.

The Tribes had only just got over this surprise, when from out the very same hut, as if it were a magician's hat, hurried Stoick the Vast, Hiccup the Third, Camicazi of the Bog-Burglars, and that weird little boy with the face-that-looked-like-a-haddock, who still had a dragon attached to his head.

The Windwalker pranced into the air, and flew joyous circles around them, so relieved and delighted was he. Even gloomy old One Eye managed a couple of happy bounces.

'MY BABY!' roared Big-Boobied Bertha, throwing wide her arms.

'Yes, Mother, another time,' said Camicazi, impatiently turning to the Eldest Elder. 'What are we waiting for? We have to start this competition RIGHT NOW.'

'Well, we've been waiting for you,' said the Eldest Elder, a little flustered. 'What happened to you... and Stoick... and Flashburn... and what was UG doing in there?'

Camacazi could be very commanding for one so small, and she could have delivered an entire lecture series on the subject of 'cheek'.

'We'll explain later. Now, we're in a hurry. Rules are rules, promises are promises, after all. This competition was supposed to start at twelve o'clock sharp on the first day of the New Year.' She picked up Hiccup's smashed ticking-thing, hanging from his pocket, and checked it, tutting. 'You're... ooh... eight

minutes late, naughty you. SOUND THE BUGLE!'
PA-A-A-A-A-A-A-A-A-A-A-A-AARPPP!

The bugle finally sounded for the start of the
swordfighting competititon to find the next King of the
Wilderwest.

'Good to see you, Stoick!' bellowed Baggybum
the Beerbelly, bashing his brother on the back in a
relieved fashion and he really meant it, for he loved his
brother, despite all the arguing. But immediately after
that touching moment he turned to the Eldest Elder,
and said, 'But they're too late for the competition,
aren't they, Eldest Elder?'

Younger brothers have not changed much, even
since the Dark Ages.

Luckily the Eldest Elder was a good sport, and
he had had a soft spot for Hiccup and Camicazi
and Fishlegs ever since he was Chief Judge in the
Swimming Race a year or so ago.*

'Good to see you, Stoick, we were worried
about you there. You four are just in time for the
competition. Hiccup, you can fight Masher here.
Fish-boy, you're against Doolally. And Cami-whatsit
can take Helly Thickarm. As for you, Stoick, well,
I'm giving you a toughie for your first match. It's the

---

* *How to Ride a Dragon's Storm* – you must read these memoirs,
otherwise you're missing out.

Goggler Twins for you I'm afraid.'

(Identical twins in the Barbaric Archipelago only counted as one person, so they had a massive advantage in swordfighting competitions.)

It says a lot for Stoick that he hadn't let his own encounter with the witch depress him too much. I suppose he had only been trapped for a day or so, whereas UG the Uglithug and Flashburn had had much longer imprisonments.

All Stoick had was a slight cramp in his swordfighting arm, which he gave a hopeful stretch with right now, and a slight hole in his belly from when he'd missed a meal or two.

And there was nothing Stoick loved more than a good FIGHT.

Stoick turned to his son, and laid an arm on his shoulder.

'Son,' he said proudly, 'Thank you.'

And then...

'Ah,' breathed Stoick the Vast, his chest puffed out, slapping his great hands together, 'BRING ON THOSE GIRLY GOGGLER TWINS AND WATCH ME TEAR THEIR HORNS OFF! BULLHEART!'

Stoick gave a whistle through his usefully-broken

front teeth. 'HERE, BOY, HERE, LET'S SHOW THESE GOGGLERS WHAT THE HOOLIGANS ARE MADE OF!'

With a happy snort, Bullheart launched himself from the top most tower and swooped down to the Battle Arena. He didn't even have to land. Stoick just ran alongside him for a couple of paces as he swooped six feet above the ground, timed his moment, leapt into the saddle, and...

'YAAAAAAARRRRR!' cried Stoick the Vast as the dragon soared upward.

Stoick the Vast was back in the saddle again.

'BACK IN THE SADDLE AGA-A-A-A-AIN, HE'S BACK IN THE SADDLE AGAIN!' cheered the happy chorus of applauding Hooligans, watching their Chieftain soar.

PAAAAAAAAAAAAAARRRP! went the bugle.

And the competition was underway.

Hiccup took off his waistcoat, and settled the Wodensfang in a good place at the edge of the Battle Arena, so he'd get a good view, with the Crown well hidden underneath him.

'Ooh, look at the colours,' blinked the

Wodensfang in wonder, looking dreamily up at the sky. 'I'd forgotten that the earth was this beautiful...'

'Guard this dragon, Toothless,' ordered Hiccup, 'he's very important.'

'Not as important as T-t-toothless,' grumbled Toothless. 'Toothless VERY important... Who IS this dragon anyway?'

Hiccup was still aching from the flight through the ice tunnels when the Masher made his first charge. So he nearly lost his balance and his duck was so awkward that it was nearly the end of the day for him right then and there.

But the Masher was over-eager. The sword whistled over Hiccup's head by a whisker, and the Masher slipped on a piece of Stickyworm slime that Flashburn had dripped on the arena as he ran over it. The Masher staggered, and Hiccup had time to recover.

'Windwalker!' called Hiccup. The Windwalker swooped down and Hiccup climbed on top of him, and they carried on the fight on dragonback for a while, which gave Hiccup the chance to catch his breath.*

It shouldn't have been an equal fight.

---

* The rules of the swordfighting competition stated that you could fight on dragonback for five minutes only during the contest.

The Masher was half a head taller than Hiccup and twice the size.

However, the Masher's brain was barely in connection with his arms and he moved like a gorilla with a hangover.

Hiccup danced around him, letting him spend all his strength flailing forwards, making wild, rushing, bull-like charges. 'STAND STILL, LITTLE RED-HAIRED BOY!' yelled the infuriated Masher, red in the face.

Within five minutes it was all over.

Exhausted, the Masher made an unwise thrust to the head, which, if it had connected, would have been the end of Hiccup. Hiccup neatly sidestepped, and parried the thrust with a sharp flick of the wrist that sent the Masher's sword spiralling out of the Masher's hand and sailing through the air.

The crowd gave a roar of delighted surprise. An upset! Stoick's weird little son had beaten the Masher!

As the loser of the fight, the Masher had to give his sword to Hiccup. Carefully, Hiccup placed the Masher's sword beside his waistcoat and the Wodensfang.

Hiccup surprised the crowd many more

266

times that afternoon.

He won swordfight after swordfight, against men twice his age, and practically twice his height. By two o'clock that afternoon there were six swords lying beside the Wodensfang on the edge of the Battle Arena; six swords all won by Hiccup.

Swordfighting was the only thing Hiccup had ever been any good at and this really was Hiccup's day. Have you ever had a moment where everything comes together?

It happened for Hiccup that afternoon. He fought as if he were out of his skin, as if he were Flashburn himself, as if he were one of the Heroes of old that he had read about in the Meathead Public Library.

He HAD to win. He knew it.

He had made the Wodensfang a promise that the Crown would not fall into the wrong hands. The future of the Archipelago, even of the dragons themselves, depended upon it. Even if the Dragon Furious did not re-appear – and Hiccup had a horrible feeling that he would – if anyone else won, they were never going to set free the dragons.

And freeing the dragons was the only thing that

was going to stop this Dragon Rebellion in its tracks.

So Hiccup fought as he had never fought before.

He was concentrating so hard that he did not even notice everyone around him falling out of the competition.

Fishlegs, of course, was disqualified in the first round, heavily hampered by Horrorcow, and Mr Pointy's blade falling out at vital moments. So he was still a Green Belt.

But Snotlout did quite well, lasted till the fifth round, where he was beaten by a gigantic Visithug (who cheated, actually). But that meant Snotlout had to be satisfied with just a Red Belt, and he was very disappointed with that.

Camicazi made it to the quarter-finals, but finally her limp got the best of her, and she was beaten by an out-of-control Madguts the Murderous. However she was still pretty happy with her Bronze Belt, for it meant that she was the youngest person ever to make FlashMaster.

But Hiccup noticed none of this. His world had shrunk to the wooden boards of the fighting area, his opponent's sword-arm, the flick and thrust of his opponent's sword.

Nothing else existed.

It was almost as if he had gone into a trance. He barely even noticed the shouting of the audience, the clash of swords, the thumping of feet on boards, the screech of watching dragons that filled the air for three long hours.

He did notice, with anxiety, that way over on his left-hand side, Alvin the Treacherous seemed to be doing well. Alvin's one-on-one swordfighting lessons with Flashburn had stood him in good stead. He had won fight after fight after fight.

Both Hiccup and Alvin made it through to the semi-finals.

Alvin's semi-final was a terrible, hard-fought match, in which Alvin nearly killed his opponent on three occasions.

The booing and hissing of the crowd told Hiccup that Alvin must be winning.

His heart sank.

Alvin as King of the Wilderwest would be the ruin of everything.

But to Hiccup's joyful astonishment, there was a sudden, astounded silence. And then the crowd around Alvin danced about and cheered wildly, as

Alvin was beaten in the dying seconds of the match.

This is too good to be true! thought Hiccup exultantly. I *can't believe this, everything is going so well, and* OOH *the witch would be cross if she wasn't in her cupboard and she saw Alvin losing...*

Hiccup did not notice who the opponent WAS who had beaten Alvin the Treacherous, though; he was too busy fighting his own match.

And he did not notice that his own fight, against Madguts the Murderous, was now being watched by the entire crowd.

He did not notice the hum of chatter. 'I always thought that boy was special! Ever since he fought that Fire-Dragon long ago,' the Vikings chattered excitedly to each other.

His concentration barely wavered when he disarmed the great Murderous with one of Flashburn's favourite moves, a Flashthrust-with-Twist-thingummy, and the crowd erupted into applause so wild that the towers around the arena seemed to shake with the noise. And the Eldest Elder declared solemnly, 'The match is won by... Hiccup Horrendous Haddock the Third!'

Camicazi shrieked, 'He's in the final!'

'Oooh!' squealed the Wodensfang. 'That's *our* guy, isn't it?'

'That's TOOTHLESS'S guy,' said Toothless grumpily. 'Not OUR g-g-guy. Toothless's Master. How many times does Toothless have to tell you? Hiccup not need another hunting-dragon. He's already got one. M-M-ME.'

For Hiccup it was like a dream, but beyond the most hopeful kind of dream that Hiccup could have dared have.

'The boy's won! The boy's won!' shouted the Vikings. The Eldest Elder fastened the FlashMaster Gold Belt around his waist and UP! he was hoisted on to great shoulders, crowds cheering round him, and reaching up to pat him on the back as he was carried to the final match, the Final, the last round.

Hiccup was in a daze of delight... almost drunk with excitement... but he came to earth with an abrupt jolt as the cheering crowds set him down in front of his last opponent.

His father.

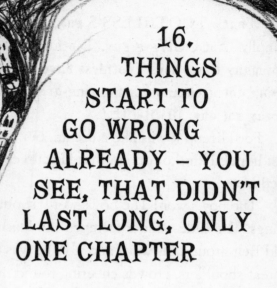

16.
THINGS
START TO
GO WRONG
ALREADY – YOU
SEE, THAT DIDN'T
LAST LONG, ONLY
ONE CHAPTER

Things had already started to go wrong,
unbeknownst to Hiccup.

He should not have locked that
witch in the cupboard.

Hiccup was young, you see, and
prone to mistakes.

When he was an older, more
experienced Hero, he would never have
done that. He would have put the witch

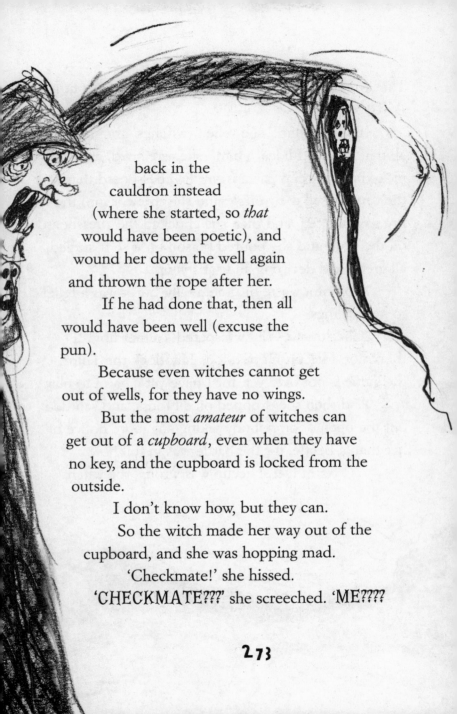

back in the
cauldron instead
(where she started, so *that*
would have been poetic), and
wound her down the well again
and thrown the rope after her.

If he had done that, then all
would have been well (excuse the
pun).

Because even witches cannot get
out of wells, for they have no wings.

But the most *amateur* of witches can
get out of a *cupboard*, even when they have
no key, and the cupboard is locked from the
outside.

I don't know how, but they can.

So the witch made her way out of the
cupboard, and she was hopping mad.

'Checkmate!' she hissed.

'CHECKMATE???' she screeched. 'ME????'

273

That wretched, creeping, lucky, burglaring, lying little ACCIDENT!

'I'll learn him!' she yelled (witches' grammar isn't all that good). 'I'll learn him!' she screamed, and she picked the Hiccup pawn from the chessboard that was the cause of all the trouble and she threw it into the fire so it melted, and then she chucked the chessboard on the floor and she poured poison on it so it sizzled, all green and decaying and satisfying.

A bit of a waste of time, really, but it was a relief to her feelings.

'Checkmate?' she whispered, calmer now. 'I think not, Hiccup Horrendous Haddock the Third, the game is not over yet, for I have yet a hand to play.'

And then she dropped on all fours, and scuttled out the open door, nobody taking any more notice of her than a beetle, for the battle was in full flow.

So in fact, Hiccup was wrong, the witch

There's nothing like a mother's sympathy when a villain is feeling low...

HAD seen Alvin being beaten in battle by Stoick, and she scurried over like a great white crab, her long hair trailing on the boards behind her, to offer her motherly sympathy and consolation.

'LOSER!'

screeched the witch.

'LOSER!'

LOSER!!

Alvin jumped as if he had been bitten, looked down, and there she was.

'I beat Madguts on points so I came *third*,' he said defensively, 'you're never satisfied, that's pretty good actually – and *you*,' he said savagely, '*you* were supposed to have got rid of Stoick and that revolting boy-nemesis of mine! I never promised I could defeat the boy-nemesis, did I? But *you* said, I'll deal with him. *You* said I have a way with clever little boys. *You* said he'll regret the day he ever was born. What happened? He's standing there, in the final, more born than ever!'

'He's immune to Vorpent poison!' screamed the witch. 'Why didn't you tell me? I said to tell me *everything*! How can I do my work unless you tell me *everything*? Being immune to Vorpent poison is a very important detail!'

'I didn't know,' replied Alvin the Treacherous, gloomily wiping some blood off his hand with the back of his sleeve. 'But it doesn't surprise me. I've been trying to kill him for years,* but he's so *tricksy*...'

'*Third!*' screamed the witch, back on that one again. 'I've got news for you, Loser-Boy! You don't get to be King of the Wilderwest if you come third!'

---

*See Hiccup's previous memoirs. How many times must I tell you!

A wicked thought came to her mid-rant. '*Actually*,' said the witch, smiling evilly. She closed her eyes, and remembered something. The witch's eyesight had improved, you see, in the months since she'd left the tree prison. And she thought she had seen something in the hut that might prove a useful weapon...

'Actually... *maybe you do*. HA! Watch out, Mr Accident, the game isn't over yet...'

And she scuttled off to see someone.

You see?

Things had taken a turn for the worse, all because Hiccup put a witch in a cupboard, and not down a well.

One little mistake is all that it takes.

17. STILL GOING WRONG

Hiccup hadn't been the only one who had fought out of his skin.

Stoick the Vast was once one of the finest swordfighters in the Archipelago, feared from east to west for his extraordinary skill with the sword.

He was a bit past it, of course, but now, being released from the witch's cupboard had given Stoick a rush of blood to the head, and he fought as if he were young again.

'The old stag has still got it, eh, Gobber?' yelled Stoick, with the joyous light of battle in his eye, swishing his sword exultantly, as he swooped down on Bullheart to high-five the hand of his old battle-companion after another incredible victory.

'HA! Stoick the Unbeatable! Stoick the Invincible! These up-and-coming young shrimps can't beat the experience of an old War Walrus like me!'

So, red in the face, swelled up with pride at his victories ('a close run thing with that Alvin guy – what a cheat the feller is'), Stoick stood before Hiccup.

When his very own son was set before him, Stoick's eyes had filled with tears.

This was too much.

He had dreamt of this moment, oh, so many times.

Stoick bellowed out the Hooligan Hoorah, echoed by all the Hooligans in the stadium. Reluctantly the other Tribes joined in. They had to admit, it was the Hooligans' moment.

'BACK IN THE SADDLE AGAIN!
HE'S BACK IN THE SADDLE AGAIN!'

King of the Wilderwest!

Stoick could not believe it. He, Stoick the Vast, was going to be King of the Wilderwest!

Hiccup stood there, quietly looking up at his father.

He thought of one of Old Wrinkly's sayings. 'Sometimes you have to stand up for what you believe in, even against those you love, and that can be harder than you think.'

He had never dreamed it would be *this* hard.

'Father,' said Hiccup wistfully, 'if you are King, will you free the dragons?'

There was such a hubbub of noise going on that at first Stoick did not hear the question, so Hiccup had to repeat it.

Stoick still had a half-smile on his face.

'Son,' he said kindly, 'the dragons can never be freed. We need them to hunt for us, to carry us into battle. The Rebellion must be put down strongly and firmly. The Rogue dragons must be taught a lesson they can never forget. It is too dangerous to free the dragons. You will understand this when you're older.'

No, I won't, thought Hiccup. *I AM older, and I still don't understand*.

That wasn't all. Stoick didn't allow human slaves on Berk. But he didn't stand up to the Uglithugs, or the Murderous, or those Tribes that *did* practise slavery. He just stood by and let it happen.

And nothing that Hiccup said was ever going to change that.

'PREPARE FOR BATTLE!' screeched the Eldest Elder. 'Make your salute to Thor!'

Hiccup and Stoick held up their swords and pledged loyalty to the great god, and the battle began.

Most Viking fathers and sons would have practised fighting each other on many previous occasions.

But Stoick was the Chief of his Tribe, and a busy man. He had never fought his son before.

So he began the fight puffed up with pride at his son's achievement in getting this far, but absolutely certain that he, Stoick, was going to win. Why wouldn't he be certain?

His son, Hiccup, was only thirteen years old.* He had shot up in height recently, but he was still kind of on the stringy side. He wasn't particularly bloodthirsty or competitive.

And why would he want to beat his own father, whom he loved and respected?

Of course Stoick thought he was going to win.

It had never occurred to Stoick that the reason that Hiccup was standing in front of him in the first place was that quietly, patiently, methodically, his gangly, weird little son had become outstandingly good at swordfighting.

Swordfighting was the only thing on the Pirate Training Programme that Hiccup had ever been any good at. Hiccup was the kind of kid who practised. So for hours and hours he had practised, quietly watching others fight, taking tips from Heroes like Humungous Hotshot and fighting against Camicazi.

He had read up about it. He knew Flashburn's swordfighting manual back to front and inside out.

---

*In fact, Hiccup had been born on the 29th of February of a Leap Year, so strictly speaking, he was still only three-and-a-quarter.

He was highly intelligent, so he could work out his opponent's weaknesses, and he didn't lose his head to temper or showing off.

And those vital inches that he had shot up recently, meant that he finally had the reach in his sword-arm to fight and beat fully-grown adults.

Hiccup himself hadn't realized this until this very moment.

Growing up happens so quick sometimes, that it catches us by surprise.

So five minutes into the fight, Stoick was very surprised indeed.

To start off with it was a pleased surprise. Stoick was a show-offy kind of fighter, and he was in a wildly confident mood. He was fighting with the Stormblade too, for he had won that off Alvin, and the Stormblade put heart into all who wielded it. So he threw his most extravagant, fancy lunges, to the roaring approval of the crowd.

And then it was a more puzzled surprise, as Hiccup parried every one of those lunges, and threw in a few of his own, one of which nearly got through Stoick's amazed guard.

And then amazement turned to growing fury.

Stoick was a Warrior, one of the finest of his age, and a Viking gets angry when he is being matched in a fight.

He forgot he fought his son.

The blood rage descended. His face turned unrecognizable with the red frenzy of battle. All thought deserted him as, yelling like a thwarted bear, he laid great swinging blows of tremendous ferocity and power about him to the left and right, back and forth.

There are many phases in a battle. Even though the stakes were high, this had started lightly, almost like a play fight, for one of the fighters was certain he would triumph, and the other was unwilling to believe that he could ever win.

But now the battle was in earnest, like a fire that suddenly caught, blazed higher than the treetops and destroyed all before it.

Accidents can happen when the blood rage descends. In that long-lost world, where knives and swords were toys and play things, accidents could happen. Friends can destroy friends, relatives can hurt relatives, in the furious heat of the temper-rash moment.

283

The witch had slithered up behind Fishlegs. He
turned and saw her standing not a few feet away, eyes
alight with greedy malevolence.

'Hisssssstory repeats itself,' hissed the witch.
'Father against son, son against father, just like it was
before... The game is not over. I shall win in the end,

Hiccup the Third. I knew I saw Death in the mice-guts... and Death it shall be, as sure as I'm Excellinor, and Excellinor is me...'

Of course Stoick was not the dread lord that Grimbeard had ever been, and Stoick would never intentionally harm a hair on his son's head... but...

Accidents can happen when the blood rage descends.

Stoick raged around Hiccup like an almighty, unstoppable storm.

Hiccup was the still point, moving only to deflect each blow, letting the storm rage around him... and absorbing Stoick's energy like a cliff absorbs the sea.

It took some time again for Stoick's puzzlement to turn to uneasiness, and uneasiness to give way to the beginnings of anxiety.

He redoubled his efforts, shot forward with a Hangman's Pass, followed by the Glancing Flick, charging, bull-like, with the Plunge for Glory.

All were met by the bright clean blade of Hiccup's sword.

Was it Stoick's imagination, or was his timing just a second or so slower, his reflexes very slightly dulled, his strength fading fast in the dying afternoon?

A battle has many phases.

Ten matches in a row is a lot even for a great Hero, especially one who has spent the last twenty-four hours folded up inside a cupboard.

Stoick tried not to feel the creeping exhaustion turning his sword-arm numb and quivering. He tried to ignore the sweat in his eyes, the protest in his aging legs as the old bones slammed down jarring on the wooden platform, the magnificent belly that had perhaps taken on a few too many beers and boars' heads in its time to keep it in the peak of physical fitness, groaning with the bruising strain and fierceness of the fight.

Stoick had always put a lot of effort into his fighting, and he was feeling it now, his shirt so drenched in sweat that it was as if he had bathed underwater, his lungs bursting, gasping, heaving for breath, his shoulders scrunched and torn in pain.

His son was barely out of breath, his face expressionless.

A Hero never surrenders! thought Stoick, fighting through the pain and—

'Owwwww...' Stoick gasped, as he pressed forward with another bruising, blustering attack, and a rip of agony in his knee sent him staggering like a toppling tree.

The old stag, you see, has old war wounds.

Long, long ago, when Stoick was performing the Quest to win Valhallarama's hand, he had injured his knee in a swordfight with a Lava-Lout.

You cannot fight Time itself, slay the minutes and the hours with your blade, wipe the bleeding seconds on your shirt.

Time cannot be fought.

Stoick tried to lunge again, but his leg would not support him. He listed to the left like a ship with a broken mast.

287

'End it, Hiccup, end it!' pleaded Stoick.

Hiccup ended it.

He stepped forward and quietly took the sword from his father's hand.

There was absolute silence in the stadium.

Time cannot be fought.

Apart from Lardtummy Lo-Watt who was so stupid that he did not realize what was going on, and was still singing:

'BACK IN THE SADDLE AGAIN, HE'S BACK IN THE SADDLE AGAIN!'

all on his own, until someone dug him in the ribs and got him to stop.

Most Vikings looked away.

There is nothing more painful than watching an old lion lose a fight, particularly to his own son.

Hiccup's face was pure sickly white.

'I'm sorry, Father,' whispered Hiccup. 'I'm sorry.'

A few of the Warriors hurried forward, and swept him up to set him in front of the Eldest Elder.

'The winner of the swordfighting competition… the Champion of Champions is…

Hiccup Horrendous Haddock the Third!' yelled the Eldest Elder.

There was still silence in the stadium.

The crowd was finding this difficult to absorb.

The rules had been followed. The gods had spoken. And *this* was who they had chosen to lead the Tribes as King? *This* skinny thirteen-year-old was to head the crushing of the Dragon Rebellion? And wasn't it all his fault in the first place? What could possibly be going on?

A Grim-bod yelled out the question that so many were thinking.

'There must be some mistake! *He* cannot be our new King!'

Angry mumblings and mutterings.

The crowd were already beginning to draw their swords. None of the Tribes really wanted a King anyway. But a weak King? A weak King was never going to hold them together.

It was a perilous moment.

But Camicazi had climbed one of the broken columns so she could be heard.

Sometimes it is helpful to have a VERY loud friend.

'*Of course* he's the King!' shouted out Camicazi. 'He has everything the King needs! Show them the Crown, Hiccup!'

Hiccup thrust the Stormblade through the loop of his belt, and the Endeavour into his scabbard, went over to where the Wodensfang was sitting on his rucksack ('**Well done**,' whispered the Wodensfang), drew out the Crown of the Wilderwest, and held it up so they all could see it.

Wow.

That made them think.

'And he's got everything else too!' bellowed Camicazi.

'Look! The Roman shield! The key-that-opens-all-locks! The arrow-from-the-land-that-does-not-exist! Grimbeard's Second-Best Sword! What else do you want? A big arrow hovering over his head saying THIS is the Heir to Grimbeard the Ghastly?'

Wow and double wow.

Added all together, this suddenly began to look pretty impressive.

Maybe there was more to this kid than met the eye. And he WAS an awesome swordfighter, particularly for his age, you had to give respect to that.

The Eldest Elder addressed the crowd.

'A promise is a promise if it is made in blood,' he reminded them. 'Your chieftains made their pledge that you would take the winner of the swordfighting competition as your King, and now you must hear him speak.'

Hiccup cleared his throat.

And now for the hard part.

18. FREEING THE DRAGONS

This was one of the most important speeches of his life, he knew it.

'Friends and fellow Vikings,' said Hiccup, 'I know that I am probably not quite the King that you expected, but destiny has decreed that I should become your King, in troubled times, facing a Dragon Rebellion. If we allow ourselves to be drawn into a war with the dragons, disaster will follow. Do we want this war? I say no.'

The Vikings murmured to each other.

They did not really want an all-out war with the dragons. Why would they? They had grown up with dragons. Their dragons slept at their firesides, they hunted fish for them, they fought by their sides in battle.

'I do not want a war with the dragons. In fact, I will do everything in my power to prevent it. I speak Dragonese. I will go to the Dragon Furious, myself, alone, and speak to him to stop this rebellion. War is not necessary! Dragons and humans can live together, I know it!

'But in order for us to stop this war, we have to

change some things about the way we live,' continued Hiccup.

He took a deep breath.

'The dragons need to be freed.'

Uproar in the castle.

Cries of 'That's just ridiculous!' and 'We depend on dragons for our livelihoods!'

Hiccup shouted above the hubbub: 'But if the war goes ahead we will have no livelihoods left! We may not even have our lives!'

The Tribes quieted again, although there were still furious mutterings and whisperings.

'Think carefully,' pleaded Hiccup. 'We are proud independent island peoples. Would we want to be chained and enslaved, forced to bow down to others as our Masters? Slavery should be banned in all its forms, for both dragons and humans.'

The Vikings were silent.

'We do not have to depend on slave and dragon labour. We are Vikings. We can stand on our own two feet. We don't have to stand by and let history just happen to us. We can take charge of our own fortune, we can improve our own futures, and stop this war before it starts. Free the dragons!'

All around the Battle Arena, the hunting-dragons were still as statues, ears back, cats' eyes watchful. Those that understood Norse were whispering in Dragonese to those that did not.

One Eye the revolutionary Sabre-Tooth Driver Dragon looked cynically down from the Second to the Left Tower. 'HA! Nice try, Hiccup my boy, but trust me, humans are incapable of change. They were pigs with whips in the past, and they'll be pigs with whips for ever.'

All around the edges of the castle, the Outcasts were prowling, like a pack of hungry wolves, ready to prove that One Eye the Sabre-Tooth was right.

But maybe One Eye was wrong.

For some reason, Hiccup's speech was striking a chord with the exhausted battle-weary Vikings. Maybe it was the long months of poor harvests and food. Maybe they were impressed by Hiccup seeming to have the will of the gods behind him. Maybe it was the thought of more fighting, and they hadn't got the heart for it.

Or maybe, just maybe, they saw that he had a point.

Who knows.

A miracle happened that day on the mountain-top.

A small miracle, perhaps just the beginning of one.

Slowly, around the arena, people began to clap.

Camicazi and Fishlegs began the applause.

Closely followed by the whole of the Bog-Burglar and Meathead Tribes, for Hiccup had done them favours in the past. And then the Hooligans, for he was one of them, and the nicer Tribes, such as the Grim-bods, and the Bashem-Oiks, and the Glums and—

Suddenly you realize that the nicer Tribes outweighed the not-so-nice.

Not the Outcasts, of course.

They didn't clap.

Nor the Visithugs or the Murderous. *They* still stood with folded arms, sullen, silent. Although, wonder of wonders, little oily Gumboil got carried away with the moment and put his black-gloved hands together (his mother was a Wanderer) until Madguts the Murderous brought him to his senses with a cuff around the ear.

'Well, shiver my wings, and bless my one good

296

eye!' wondered One Eye the old Sabre-Tooth. 'What a wonder to be wrong! Two hundred years I've served these humans, two hundred years... and I never thought they'd surprise me...'

Close by, Stoick lifted his drooping head.

'I knew it!' whispered Camicazi, eyes shining. 'He *is* the King after all! I knew it!'

If only *THIS* was THE END

19. TURNING THEIR BACKS

It would have been good if this was *THE END*.

But unfortunately this is a Hiccup story, and if I have said it once, I have said it a hundred times: this is the story of becoming a Hero the Hard Way.

We've become so caught up in listening to Hiccup's speech that we've forgotten about the witch.

All the while that Hiccup was talking, and the Vikings were listening, the witch had been busy.

Scuttling and slaloming through the hairy legs of the watching crowd, like a bony white dog, searching, searching.

Looking for someone.

And she found him.

Whisper, whisper, whisper in Snotlout's ear.

It's all about timing you see. That's what the witch had learnt from her twenty years in the tree trunk. And on this occasion, her timing was impeccable.

Just at that moment, when it was all in the balance, when it looked like, against all odds, that everything might just go right in the end after all, someone threw a stone.

Snotlout threw the stone and Snotlout was an exceptionally good shot.

The stone connected with Hiccup's helmet with a bright clear ring, and it fell to the ground.

Hiccup gave an appalled gasp and tried to put his hand to his forehead.

Too late.

The Eldest Elder's quick old eyes saw something there, and his knobbly old arm reached out, and slowly, sternly, he brought down Hiccup's hand to reveal...

... the Slavemark.

You see, that was what the witch had seen, earlier, in the hut.

Hiccup had done a wonderful job of keeping the Slavemark secret over the years.*

But when Toothless crept under Hiccup's helmet, in that moment that he lifted it up from Hiccup's forehead, before letting it fall again, the witch had seen the Mark that was hiding underneath.

The Slavemark was the ultimate mark of shame in the Archipelago.

It meant instant banishment from your Tribe, and a life lived for ever in slavery.

The crowd let out a cry of horror.

'The boy is a slave!' yelled a Murderous. 'No wonder he wanted us to free the dragons, and the human slaves as well! He is a slave himself!'

---

*To find out how Hiccup got the Slavemark read *How to Ride a Dragon's Storm*.

'We have been tricked!' called out a Visithug.

Roars of indignation and shaken fists.

'Silence!' cried the Eldest Elder, his white beard all a-quiver. And he turned to Stoick, aghast. 'How is it that your son has the Slavemark? Surely you are not trying to foist upon us a leader who is a *slave*?'

Stoick was barely able to take this in. 'But... but... this isn't possible... Hiccup, how could this be? There is some mistake, surely?'

Hiccup had put his hand up to his forehead again, almost as if he was hoping that the Mark wasn't really there.

'I was given the Mark by the Wanderers long ago on the slave ship when I went to America,' explained Hiccup.

He brought his hand down again. 'It was an accident... but there is no shame in this, Father...'

He had lost the goodwill of the crowd, however.

It was all a question of timing.

In that time, in that place, a person with the Slavemark could never be a Chief, let alone a King.

'Oh dear, oh dear, oh dear, oh dear,' sighed the Eldest Elder.

This was all very confusing.

'Hiccup cannot be the King,' ruled the Eldest Elder. 'He is disqualified because he has the Slavemark. You, then, shall be the next King of the Wilderwest, Stoick, for you were the runner-up in the sword-fighting competition.'

'Stoick should be banished too!' came a hissing voice and the witch Excellinor rose, almost as if she were floating, on to the platform.

She held up her iron-tipped fingernails.

'These are surgeon's fingers,' hissed the witch. 'What do we do when we meet a cancer, a tumour, or a canker in our bodies?' she screamed. 'We rip it out, we tear it from our flesh, so that the rest of the body may have a chance to live! So it is,' sneered the witch, and she snuffled a little, like a dog, 'so it is with *runts*. What is the motto of the Hooligan Tribe, Stoick?'

'Only the strong can belong,' said Stoick, who had turned very white.

'None of you idiots know your history do you?' purred the witch. 'Hiccup is the name given to RUNTS in the Horrendous Haddock family, isn't it, Stoick?

'Your son,' the witch spat out the words as if they were an exceptionally nasty taste in her mouth, 'your

302

nasty, puny, *odd* little son, was pronounced a runt by the Naming Dame, wasn't he, Stoick? You should have set him out to sea, according to the Law, shouldn't you? But you DID NOT! Deny it if you can, Stoick the Vast!'

Stoick could not.

Thirteen years before, the Naming Dame had indeed pronounced Hiccup a runt. It was a private ceremony, so only he and Valhallarama knew this secret. But he and Valhallarama had wanted a child so very, very badly. They had argued to themselves that the Naming Dame must have been wrong. They kept their baby, and in so doing, they broke one of the most sacred Laws of the Archipelago.

The Hooligans had watched Hiccup growing up, watched and wondered why he was so skinny and ordinary-looking. But never had they suspected that their own, most respected, Chief would have broken the Law in this way.

Many among them had painfully said goodbye to their own infants, suppressed their personal feelings for the good of the Tribe. Was it possible that Stoick, their great leader, had not done the same?

And all around the amphitheatre the sky

seemed to darken.

The dragons were skulking now, still as statues. They sensed that something bad was about to happen.

The witch gave a shrieking cackle like a swooping bird of prey.

She had won! She had won! She knew she had won.

'You see!' she triumphed. 'The gods have marked him out despite his father's treachery and weakness, the gods have marked him out by giving him the Slavemark!

'Turn your backs, O Ye Tribes of the
Archipelago!' screamed the witch. 'Turn your backs on
this wickedly weak Chieftain and his spawn of oddity.
Turn your backs for ever and all may yet be well!'

You see how close the line is, between triumph
and disaster?

The Tribes had no choice, really.

One by one they turned their backs on Stoick
and his son, some slower than others, but they all
turned, even Baggybum the Beerbelly, and Bertha
of the Bog-Burglars, and last of all, Stoick's warrior
companion, who had fought a hundred battles by his
side, Gobber the Belch.

Turn Your Backs, O Ye
Tribes of the Archipelago!

He had tears in his eyes, and a heart as heavy as a stone, but he turned nonetheless.

Even Camicazi, though she did not turn, stood frozen as a statue, paralysed with horror at her idol Hiccup, shattered.

The Slavemark! How *could* he have the Slavemark?

He wasn't the perfect hero either, any more than Flashburn.

Only one person spoke up.

That person was Fishlegs.

'*Horrorcow*,' whispered Fishlegs, very dignified, in his dragon's ear. '*We're safe now. Please release me. I don't want people to laugh...*'

The vegetarian dragon swallowed hard. She was still frightened, but for the first time in three weeks she untangled her talons from Fishlegs's shoulders, crept down to his feet, and let… him… go.

Fishlegs got to his feet on trembling legs.

'*I* do not turn,' he said though his voice was
shaking. '*I* do not turn.'

'And who are *you*?' scoffed the witch. '*You're* just
a runt, like the Hiccup himself!'

'I may be a runt,' said Fishlegs, 'but I am a
runt saved by Fate and the gods, so I have my say
nonetheless. And Hiccup is still *my* King,
Slavemark or no Slavemark.'

Fishlegs walked towards
Hiccup.

Fishlegs reached around
his neck and took from it his
most prized possession.

It was the lobster-claw
necklace that had been
found beside the baby
Fishlegs in the basket that

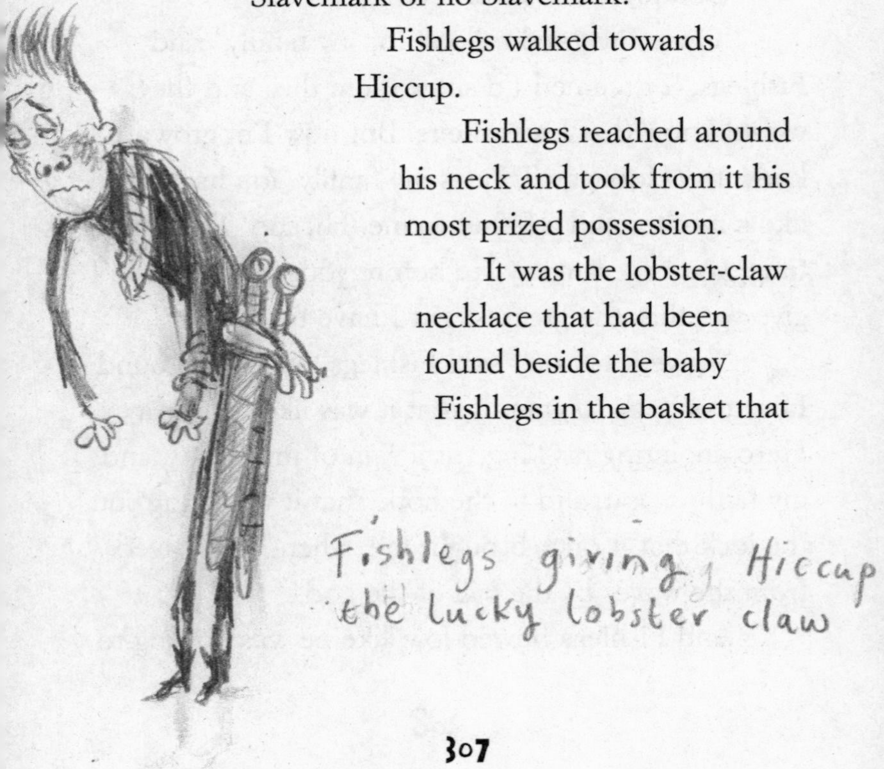

Fishlegs giving Hiccup
the lucky lobster claw

was washed up on the Long Beach, thirteen long years before.

It wasn't exactly gold and jewels, just an old lobster claw, but Hiccup knew what it meant.

'You can't give me this, Fishlegs!' said Hiccup. 'It's the only thing you own that came from your parents!'

Fishlegs spoke very formally, as if he were a grown-up.

Goodbyes are solemn things.

'Once I wanted to look for my family,' said Fishlegs, 'I dreamed I'd show them this, and they would know that I was theirs. But now I'm grown I know the Hooligan Tribe is my family. You have been like a mother and a father to me, Hiccup. Time after time, you have put my life before your own. And so I give you this, the greatest gift I have to give.

'I give it to you,' said Fishlegs, putting it round Hiccup's neck so grandly that it was like he was a Hero anointing his king, 'as a sign of my loyalty, and my faith in you, and in the hope that it will bring you the luck that it once brought me, when I was saved from the waves by the will of the gods.'

And Fishlegs bowed low, like he was bowing to

his lord, and backed away, as one must when one is in the royal presence.

'Sweet...' purred the witch. 'Very sweet. Stop, my eyes are tearing up...' And she took the Eldest Elder's stick, and jabbed the backing Fishlegs with it, so that he fell over. 'Back, back, you fish-legged freak-boy, you cannot go where he must go now... *lucky for you...*'

Hiccup felt the lobster claw round his neck. Fishlegs's faith in him had given him strength.

'No!' he shouted. 'You are wrong! Our Fate is not what we look like, it is not written down in the stars, it is not the Mark upon us! Our Fate is *who we are*!'

'We shall see...' hissed the witch. 'We shall see... NOW... *your* Fate shall be decided by your new King... Who could that be, now? If the runt is disqualified... and the runt's father too... Why bless my very eyes and whiskers, the one who came third, must be the King! The new King must be...'

All her life the witch had waited for this moment, planned for it, schemed for it, killed for it, plotting and spinning her webs in the darkness, and now at last here it was. Fate was her friend after all these years.

The witch spread wide her arms like the wings of a bat, and screamed up to the heavens.

'THE NEW KING IS ALVIN THE TREACHEROUS, BLOOD OF MY BLOOD, AND BONE OF MY BONE!'

And then she turned to Hiccup.

'Checkmate, I think you'll find, Hiccup Horrendous Haddock the Third.'

CHECKMATE, I think you'll find, Hiccup Horrendous Haddock the Third.

20. THE TRIUMPH OF THE TREACHEROUS

'Dear, oh dear, oh dear,' whispered the Wodensfang, talking to himself. 'Well, that didn't take long, did it? The Crown has fallen into the wrong hands even quicker than last time...' The Wodensfang didn't seem as downcast as he should have been. 'But Hiccup IS the Heir, I know that now, there is no doubt about it...'

The sky was very dark now, deep with thunderclouds so close above their heads it felt like you could reach out and touch them.

Everyone felt in a bewildered way that the world had turned upside-down. They had just banished Stoick the Vast, who most people agreed was a thoroughly nice chap, an old burglar of course, but generally thought to be a good Viking and one of them.

And now the Chief of the Outcasts was about to be made their King.

What was going on?

They had been tricked but they couldn't quite

put their hairy fingers on HOW it had happened.

The dragons were tense, their cats' eyes gleaming in the darkness, down on their haunches, muscles poised for flight.

Only minutes ago they were in touching distance of freedom. But a minute can be a long time.

A new lord for the Vikings meant a new lord for themselves, too. What would it mean? Who was this Treacherous human, and what did he stand for?

Alvin threw back his cloak and strode to the centre of the Battle Arena, swelling with triumph.

He had been a handsome man once, and you could still see that in the ruins of his face, scarred like a fallen angel. You could still see that in the grace and elegance of the ironic bow he made to Hiccup.

'I am only sorry,' he smiled, as charming as if he were at an evening feast, 'that we did not meet in battle one last time, Hiccup Horrendous Haddock the Third. But I am sure you are not a poor loser.' His voice turned to iron. 'Hand over the Stormblade, and the King's Things.'

One by one Hiccup handed them over.

The Stormblade. The Roman shield. The ticking-thing. The key-that-opens-all-locks. The arrow-from-the-land-that-does-not-exist. The bracelet with the ruby heart's stone. The Crown. And last of all…

'The sword, Hiccup. Hand over the sword.'

The Dragon Jewel was hers, she knew it, for the sword would point the way.

'Oh yes, it is the triumph of the Treacherous at last, for you, Alvin, you are King,' and with that the witch went down upon her knees and knelt before her son, the new King.

Graciously, Alvin allowed her to kiss his hand.

You see how sometimes it is not clear what story we are telling from the outset? For the story we have been a part of, it turns out, has not just been about the making of a Hero, but also the making of a villain.

The Alvin that we first met, many books and years ago, was not the same terrible man who was now about to be crowned upon the castle that once was Flashburn's. When first we met him, he was a charming, sneaking, elegant sort of fellow, barely able to hold his own in a swordfight.

Since then, dreadful things have happened to Alvin, all his own fault of course, but he has suffered nonetheless. Suffering can, of course, make a man a better person – but with Alvin it went the other way, and it had made him far, far worse. With every ghastly experience he lost a little more of his humanity along with his hair, his leg, his nose, his eye…

And now he stands, muscled, hardened, brutal and merciless, a truly awful man indeed to wield the power he would hold from now on.

Alvin took the Crown, put it on his head and turned to face the still-silent crowd.

The witch gave a sigh of the purest satisfaction.

'And now,' Alvin said silkily, and almost casually gesturing to Hiccup, 'put this slave-boy and his father into chains, and throw them to the Uglithug Slavelands, never to return. Put the Mark upon the father too, as a sign of how he betrayed his own people.

ruby stone heart's –

Roman shield

icking-thing crown ↓

'Friends, Barbarians and Vikings!' he yelled. He thrust the Endeavour in the air.

'Let me tell you what kind of King *I* am going to be… I have not come to set your dragons FREE,' sneered Alvin the Treacherous. 'Are we to just sit back and let them destroy our world? I say no, and again no! From now on I declare WAR of the most dreadful and bloody kind on all wild dragons.

← key
← Grimbeard's Second-Best Sword
← arrow

NOW. Let me tell you what kind of King I am going to be…

All wild dragons must be killed on sight, with our Northbows and our axes, and the most fanciful instruments of human ingenuity. We shall seek out their nests, set fire to their habitats, destroy their eggs and their hibernating young...'

Alvin was drunk on power now. 'And as for the domestic dragons,' he purred gloatingly (Alvin had never liked dragons of any kind, and here was his chance for revenge), 'dangerous times call for drastic measures. All domestic dragons shall be CHAINED at all times, unless they are doing a job for a human. They shall spend their nights in cages. Any hint of rebellion, and they will be killed on the spot.'

There was a silence as these words sank in.

This was too much even for the meaner Tribes, the Murderous and the Visithugs.

One person clapped.

The witch.

'HE cannot rule over us!' cried Camicazi.

'Oh, I'm sorry,' purred the witch. 'Don't you remember? A promise is a promise if it is made in blood...'

'No!' shouted Hiccup. 'No! You mustn't do this! You'll anger our dragons into joining the Rebellion...

They'll turn against us…'

'Coward,' sneered Alvin the Treacherous.

'Keep calm!' cried Hiccup to the dragons in Dragonese, as all around him he could hear the dragons beginning to scream and snarl. 'Not even the tough Tribes agree with him… They just need a bit of time to see sense… Don't do anything stupid… Nobody do anything stupid…'

But it was too late.

One Eye the Sabre-Tooth Driver Dragon leapt through the crowd like a great white lion, scattering Vikings to all sides. He threw back his head and roared, 'How dare you, human worm? Us dragons were not born for chains! I, for one, am joining the Rebellion, and you shall be my first victim!'

He opened his mouth to bite Alvin in half.

'Seize him!' screeched Alvin, and ten or twenty burly Vikings tackled the great dragon and pinned him to the ground.

SEIZE HIM!!

Alvin drew the Stormblade.

'*You*, you great white elephant,' smiled Alvin, his own mean one eye smiling into the furious, struggling dragon's one eye, 'shall be the first to die... I shall christen this Battle Arena with your foul dragon blood and thus the War begins... But first I will make you blind...'

And you shall be the first to die, you great white elephant

'No,' wept Hiccup, unable to bear it. 'No, no, no...'

Alvin raised his sword to bring it down on the

helpless dragon's head.

But just as he was about to bring it down, the ground beneath Alvin's feet seemed to buckle and tremble.

And behind Alvin's head, the witch's fortune-telling hut, that little, sinister dwelling... *exploded* in front of the Vikings' eyes.

Sending bits of brick and cobwebs and destiny charts and birds bones, and the whole messy morass of the witch's room showering all over the crowd.

By complete coincidence the entire gunky stinking contents of one of the witch's cauldrons landed on her head, along with the sign saying Fortunes Told, Futures Improved.

And a great gush of fire shot through the hole where the hut once was, two hundred feet up into the air, as if someone had struck fire instead of oil, like a great geyser of flame.

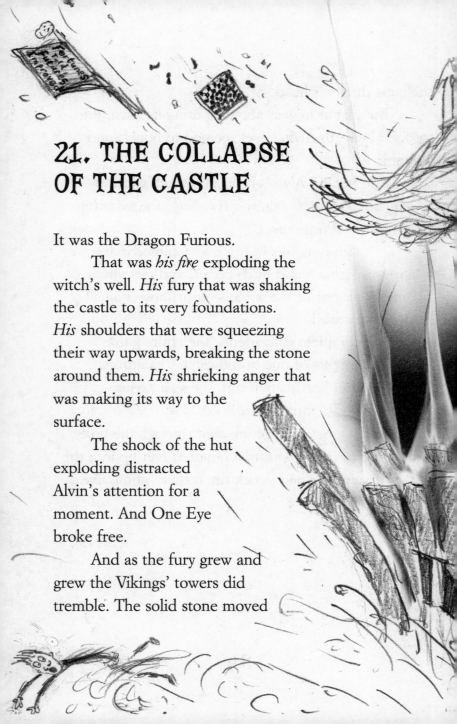

21. THE COLLAPSE OF THE CASTLE

It was the Dragon Furious.

That was *his fire* exploding the witch's well. *His* fury that was shaking the castle to its very foundations. *His* shoulders that were squeezing their way upwards, breaking the stone around them. *His* shrieking anger that was making its way to the surface.

The shock of the hut exploding distracted Alvin's attention for a moment. And One Eye broke free.

And as the fury grew and grew the Vikings' towers did tremble. The solid stone moved

beneath their feet
as if it had turned
to ocean. Great
cracks appeared in
the ancient castle,
like the splitting
and breaking of an
iceberg, lumps of
stone raining down from
the shaking battlements.
The edges of the hole where the
hut had stood just moments before fell
in on themselves, as the Dragon
Furious burrowed upwards with his
powerful claws. His great fountain
of fire and smoke went shooting
up hundreds of feet into the air,
sending dragons and humans
scurrying and fleeing in
all directions.

The gigantic creature's shoulders shook aside the stone as if it were water, his head burst through the gaping hole in the floor, and up, up, up he rose like a living earthquake, splaying one claw on the edge of the hole and heaving his body slowly upwards.

With a last shrugging scream, he leapt free of the stone and earth, and into the air, his spreading wings bursting a trembling tower into pieces, his mighty wingspan darkening the sun like an enormous cloud.

Petrified, the Vikings stared upwards at their terrifying enemy.

And for the first time, they realized, too late, that while they were absorbed in their own human drama, and even the sentries at the castle were watching the battle for the Crown of the Wilderwest, dragons had been creeping across the sky towards the castle.

Hostile dragons. Rogue and Red-Rage dragons. And now the sky above was dark with dragons.

The Dragon Furious shot his flame to left and right in a screaming fiery river.

"Join the Red-rage and rebel, Brother-Dragons, rebel!"

Now, if *Hiccup* had still been King of the
Wilderwest, the domestic dragons would have replied
to the Dragon Furious that they were already free,
thank you very much, and the great Dragon Rebellion
might have been stopped before it started.

You cannot rebel if you are already free.

You see how near Hiccup was to triumph.

So near and yet so far.

As it was, all around the castle, the dragons
that had been quiet as cats became a nest of hissing
serpents. Out sprang their claws, their teeth like
knives, the hot fire flamed.

came the trumpeting tones of One Eye.

"Rebel, brother-dragons, rebell!"
"The humans are our mortal enemies
now! Join us, O my Brothers, in the
Red-Rage and rebel!"

All around the stadium, the echo came, quiet at
first, the whisper went,

"Rebel..."

then louder still and louder.

"*Rebel*" they spat, "*Rebel!*" they hissed,

And with one accord, like a dragon cloud, they turned upon their Masters.

"Rebel, Rebel, Rebel!"

With surprised yells, the Vikings drew their weapons to defend themselves, as dragons leapt upon their backs, lion-claws raking, and the hot fire burnt their unprotected skin.

All around Hiccup the battle raged.

Dragon against human.

The air was filled with the screams of the attacking dragons, the Vikings barely able to believe that they were being fought by the very same creatures who had fed from their hands and slept at their firesides. It was as if some alien wild spirit had got into them, as if they had been cornered by a previously unsuspected enemy.

Stoick, abandoned by his captors but still unarmed, was faced by his own dragon, Bullheart, crouched down low like a tiger about to spring, growling deep in his throat, the anger glands thick about his neck.

'DOWN, BULLHEART, DOWN!' commanded Stoick.

But Bullheart did not appear to hear him. He kept his steady cat's eyes on Stoick as he crept slowly forward. He seemed to be growling, but if Stoick could speak Dragonese he would have recognised the following words:

"Join the Red-Rage and REBEL
MakE red your claws with human blood,
Obliterate the Human Filth ...
Torch the HUMans like a wood ...
The Rebellion is coming. "

Stoick swallowed.

'Down, Bullheart,' he said. Bellowing did not seem to be doing its usual magic, for the dragon crept on regardless.

"Slake your thirst with human tears,"
Do not spare the human child,
Incinerate the human pest,
The Dragontime is Coming."

'DOWN!' bellowed Stoick desperately.

As with a mighty roar his old war-horse of
a dragon leapt towards him, mouth agape, talons
pointed, nostrils flaring, throat working to release the
deadly fire.

And all would not have gone well for Stoick if
Viking arrows were not already flying through the air
as the humans defended themselves, and if one of
these arrows had not pierced the leg of the charging
Bullheart, felling him to the ground with a yowl of pain
and fury.

The castle was falling fast now.

Three of the towers were down. A fourth was
tottering, and the dragons were attacking with such
force and savagery, and the Vikings were so
unprepared for the sudden onslaught of the castle,
that their defeat seemed inevitable.

Here the flames scorching and wrecking, warriors

fleeing with screams, firing their arrows over their shoulders. There, the Dragon Furious, breathtaking in his enormity, tearing up the armoury where some unfortunate Vikings had fled for shelter, or blasting the Warriors into the next world with a river of flame. All around the roar of dragon and the sickening thud of axe blade or sword sinking into flesh.

There was a constant rain of arrows, a steady drift of spears, and swords melted and twisted by the hail of fire. The Vikings had got hold of the catapults and were using these against the dragons, causing terrible injuries. But the Vikings were not winning. Hiccup could see this, even as he squinted through the choking clouds of smoke, panting, desperate.

They were losing.

'I can't let this happen,' whispered Hiccup, 'I can't let this happen...' But what could he do? His hands were bound with rope, the castle was falling down, the dragons were killing the humans all around. What could he do?

'Toothless!' shouted Hiccup into the uncaring air. 'Toothless! Please come here, I need you! Toothless!'

22. RED-RAGE

Toothless was closer than Hiccup realized.

The Red-Rage had entirely overtaken him, like a powerful drug takes hold of a feeble mind. The ancient primeval anger of the wild world took him over so crazily that he lost his sight in the dizzying force of it, and it numbed the sensible parts of his brain. Drunk with power and fury, he attacked the discarded shoe of a fleeing Viking, under the misguided belief that it was a real human child.

'RED-RAGE!'

he squeaked,
ripping out the shoelaces.

'RED-RAGE!!'

he screamed,
shredding the leather into tangled rags of ribbons.

'Hunt the human and throw him to the fire!!'

he screeched as he tore out the sole
and blasted it with flames.

What was it about
Hiccup's voice that cut
through the fog of fury and
made Toothless turn and stare,
his mouth full of smoking shoe
leather? The mist of the Red-
Rage that had descended on the
little dragon lifted as if by magic. Toothless turned.
He dropped the shoe. He flew to where Hiccup was
standing, bound with ropes.

'Toothless!' exclaimed Hiccup. 'Quick! Bite my
ropes and find the Windwalker!'

'Do this! D-d-do that!' grumbled the little
dragon. 'Toothless not your s-s-servant...'

But he bit through the ropes with one quick
snap of his sharp little jaws, and he flew to find the
Windwalker with none of his usual laziness.

The Windwalker was flying around in confused circles some distance away, searching for Hiccup. The Red-Rage had not taken him over, but it had thoroughly disorientated him, interrupting his radar, and what with that, and the smoke, and dodging the arrows and spears, he was looping the loop, and bumping into other dragons, and accidentally chasing his own tail.

'Hiccup needs us!' squeaked Toothless, forgetting to be cool, and the Windwalker followed the little dragon, weaving expertly through the aerial battlefield, and crash-landed beside Hiccup in an untidy scramble.

Hiccup leapt on the Windwalker's back in the nick of time, for a Tonguetwister was lunging his way, and the Windwalker climbed up, up, up into the air.

What can I do? What can I do? What can I do?

Hiccup guided the Windwalker down for a moment to the edge of the Battle Arena, and leant over to pick up the Wodensfang and his waistcoat.

'What are you bothering with him for?' complained Toothless. 'We don't n-n-need *him*!'

'Ah, I knew I wasn't wrong about you!' exclaimed the Wodensfang in delight. 'You ARE the Heir after all!'

330

But Hiccup's view from the Windwalker's back, as the black dragon swam higher and higher through the air, gave him a full view of the desperate tragedy of the situation.

The castle was collapsing even further now, caving in on itself, crumbling into the great hole in the centre caused by the eruption of the Dragon Furious. The great dragon himself was right in the centre, breathing out flame almost continuously.

Practically all the Warriors in the Archipelago had gathered at the castle, don't forget, so they were a mighty army indeed, and they were fighting back the dragons with enormous bravery. To the left he could see Snotlout, admittedly fighting with terrific skill and valour, urging on the Hooligans as if he were Chief already.

In the centre was the fiercest fighting, for there was Alvin the Treacherous, and the majority of dragons were trying to get the sword Endeavour. Alvin was surrounded by a ring of Tribesmen, fighting to defend their new King, and he was giving a good account of himself, the Stormblade fixed into his attachment, the Endeavour in the other hand.

To the right, the Bog-Burglars had got hold of a

catapult and were constantly re-loading, blasting great holes in the dragon attack.

Things were looking dreadful, nonetheless. The casualties on both sides were horrific in number. And the Vikings were losing, Hiccup could see that, for they were unprepared, and they had no means of joining in the aerial combat now their own dragons had deserted them.

The Red-Rage was terrifyingly loud now, a dreadful drumming sound that no human being should ever have to hear, a jungle noise that chilled the blood and choked the heart and sent the hairs on the scalp tingling with electric horror.

They're going to destroy each other, thought Hiccup. *But what can I do? What can I do? What can I do? I'm just one person, what can I do?*

Into Hiccup's frazzled brain there floated Old Wrinkly's words: 'And then the world will need a Hero, and it might as well be you...'

'Windwalker!' Hiccup whispered into his riding-dragon's ear, 'Windwalker! Head towards that patch of light over there!'

There was a small clearing in the clouds, and narrowly missing a couple of arrows, Windwalker flew

332

right into it. All around was blackness and smoke, but in that tiny patch of bright blue sky, the sun glinted dazzlingly off Windwalker's shining wings, and Hiccup's dragonskin fire-suit, so that they were clearly visible from down below.

A ray blinked down into Camicazi's eye, and Camicazi saw him, though she was fighting hard, and despite the fact you could only see the outline of a human mounted on a dragon's back, she knew that it was him.

'Hiccup!' she whispered with passionate relief, forgetting that he had the Slavemark, and just grateful he was there. 'Hiccup! He's going to save us, I know he will, he'll have some clever plan...'

To tell the truth, Hiccup had absolutely no plan at all, but as he hung there in the crack of light, the only piece of hope in a dark and dreadful world, a glimmer of an idea popped into his head.

'DRAGONS!' yelled Hiccup. 'DRAGONS!!!!! FORGET ABOUT THE SWORD, FOR I HAVE THE JEWEL ALREADY IN MY HAND!'

He held up his clenched fist, way over his head.

Dragons' hearing is so acute they can hear the nanodragons laughing to one another in the grasses.

They heard this all right.

Slowly, the Dragon Furious turned its mighty head towards the boy as if he were an annoying insect buzzing above his head. The dragon's jaws were already dipped scarlet with human blood. His eyes narrowed.

Truth or lies?

'It'ss not true...' he hissed. 'Not true, the boy lies, I know it by my own forked tongue...'

He narrowed his eyes further, squinting beyond the light, beyond the boy, seeking, seeking into the future, his mind processing the possibilities like an endless game of chess...

Something that he saw there made him hiss. 'And yet...'

And yet.

'CATCH THE BOY!!!!' screamed the Dragon Furious. 'CHASE HIM! HUNT HIM! TEAR HIM FROM THE SKY! WHATEVER YOU DO, DON'T LET HIM GET AWAAAAAAYYYYYY!!!'

A thousand dragons paused and held their fire. A thousand dragons turned their heads and their narrowing yellow, green, and blue cats' eyes, and focused them on the boy like they were arrows and he was the target.

Toothless, hovering some considerable distance above Hiccup's head, gave a yelp of horror, put his little claws together as if he were praying, folded back his wings, and dived ten feet downwards into the front of Hiccup's shirt, joining the Wodensfang down there.

'Fly, Windwalker,' Hiccup whispered into the Windwalker's ear. 'Fly Windwalker, fly... Fly like you've never flown before...'

23. FLY, WINDWALKER, FLY

One second the Vikings were fighting a losing battle.

The next, thousands and thousands of dragons let out a simultaneous scream.

The entire dragon army, the Dragon Furious himself, and dragons in their thousands, flew in screaming blood-lust pursuit after the boy on the dragon.

The Windwalker let out a petrified scream like that of a trapped fox. He buzzed around in crazy circles in the patch of light, looping the loop –

as if that was helpful.

'Fly, Windwalker, fly,' whispered Stoick from down below, forgetting for a moment that he was a slave, and willing his son on. 'Fly, or they'll tear him to pieces...'

With a dreadful whinnying snort, the Windwalker came to his senses and shot off in a random direction.

Panting, shocked, blackened, the Vikings found their enemy had deserted them as suddenly as they had attacked.

Craning their necks upwards, they could see the entire dragon army up there in the firmament, swarming from horizon to horizon, from sky tip to sky tip, like a swarm of angry hornets chasing a tiny little gnat.

The gnat that was Hiccup dashed this way and that, up, down, zig-zagging, looping, with the entire murderous swarm zooming after him, breaking up as they doubled back on themselves, re-forming, closing in, droning the chilling Red-Rage as they flew.

'He's going to tire!' whispered Camicazi, hopping from foot to foot in anxiety, 'they'll catch him when he tires!'

What an unpleasant smile was on the face of Alvin the Treacherous as he stared upwards into the sky. 'And that,' he drawled, '*that* is the end of Hiccup Horrendous Haddock the Third, by the ghost of my good right hand it is...'

Alvin turned and faced his new subjects, back straight, face stern, every inch a King.

'Vikings, we are now at WAR! War outright, bloody and terrible. Shall our brother comrades lying dead about us, ripped and scorched to death by the talons and the fire of these vermin, shall they all have died in vain?'

Cries of 'No!' from the furious, devastated Vikings.

'We shall not sleep, brother Vikings, we shall not close our eyes. We shall return to our islands and build weapons of war so gruesome and so murderous that these dragons could not even dream of them. We shall not rest till every forked-tongue crocodile lies dead and wingless at our feet. Extinction, brother Vikings! We are aiming for extinction!'

You must not blame the Vikings' reaction here, readers.

Remember that all around them were the sad bodies of their fallen comrades. Remember the shock of their domestic dragons rebelling against them. They were grieved and shocked out of their normal senses.

'From now on,' yelled Alvin, 'you must kill every dragon on sight, no questions asked! Swear to me that you will.'

The Vikings swore that terrible oath.

This is the way that wars begin.

And that was how the last Great War between humans and dragons finally came about. And how Alvin, loathed by many, became the leader of the human army. Wars make strange and terrible leaders.

'To the boats!' yelled Alvin. 'Before the dragons return!'

And then, in an aside to Bellicose, the leader of the Bashem-Oiks: 'Take this Stoick to the Uglithug Slavelands. Be sure to put the Mark upon him, like that traitor his son.'

And to the Hooligans: 'I declare the next Chief of the Hooligan Tribe should be this Snotface Snotlout, in honour of his noble act exposing the treachery of Stoick and his son.'

'Here, I say!' protested Baggybum the Beerbelly, outraged to be overlooked, even though Snotlout was his own son. '*I'm* the next in line to the Chiefdom!'

Alvin smiled his horrid smile. 'What this day has shown is that you old fat men are past it. *Snotlout* is the Chief, and anyone who objects will follow Stoick to the Slavelands.'

So Snotlout had what he had desired all along, the Chiefdom of the Hooligan Tribe. His chest swelled up like a cockerel's.

I knew it, he thought to himself exultantly. *I knew it had to be me... I knew I couldn't be this brilliant for nothing...*

He couldn't repress a smile of infinite smugness, one that lit up his pimply face, as he twirled the Flashcut in one hand.

His first act as Chief showed off Snotlout's character in its most unpleasant light.

'Move along there, Baggybum,' he ordered his

father, self-importantly. 'Don't dawdle. You heard the King. To the boats!'

So that was a sad procession of Vikings, scrambling over the devastated edges of their once-impregnable castle, down the mighty cliffs to their half-broken ships. They carried their dead and injured on makeshift stretchers as they retreated back to their homelands, ready to make war on the entire dragon race.

Camicazi, hurrying along with the Bog-Burglars, stopped a moment beside Fishlegs, standing still as a stone, tears pouring down his face, looking down at Hiccup's helmet lying at his feet on top of the rubble.

'Why are you crying?' asked Camicazi in surprise.

'Hiccup is dead,' whispered Fishlegs.

'No he's not,' said Camicazi briskly. 'You gave him your lucky lobster claw, didn't you?'

'What use is a lucky lobster claw! He was being hunted by the entire Dragon Rebellion!' said Fishlegs.

'He'll think of something,' said Camicazi. 'He always does. Listen, Fishlegs,' Camicazi put a hand on Fishlegs's shoulder, 'you can't despair now. I was wrong to turn my back on Hiccup with the others.

We must be STRONG Fishlegs, we must hope for the BEST!

You stood by him. So you can't give up on him now. Now we have to hope for the best, and trust that Hiccup will save us from the dragons.'

'How can he possibly save us?' asked Fishlegs. 'Even if he survives, from now on he's an Outcast, an exile!'

There are some people who really come into their own in a crisis, and Camicazi was one of them. The joyous light of battle was in her eye. She whistled breezily through her front teeth. Suddenly she looked much older, too.

'Yup, everything is upside-down, isn't it?' said Camicazi. 'But Hiccup has *already* saved us, hasn't he? If he hadn't drawn off the dragons, we'd have been massacred. Be strong, Fishlegs! Be strong and hope for the best!'

Camicazi hurried off to join her own Tribe.

Fishlegs took off his broken glasses, polished them, and jammed them firmly back on his blackened nose. He picked up Hiccup's helmet, put it on his head instead of his own, and squared his shoulders. He knew that he was in for a bad time now that Snotlout was Chief of the Hooligan Tribe, but he straightened his back nonetheless.

However bad his own situation, Hiccup's would be infinitely worse.

He would be strong. He would hope for the best.

He would be strong.
He would hope
for the best.

24. THE BOY HUNT

Camicazi was right.

Hiccup needed all the hope and courage that he could get.

Being pursued by the entire dragon army was the most terrifying thing that had happened to him in his whole life – and Hiccup had had some terrifying experiences.

Screaming through the sky, crouched flat on

the Windwalker's back, his arms around the dragon's neck, he felt his end was coming. He couldn't get his feet in the stirrups so he was clinging on with arms so cold they were practically statues. Behind him the stupefyingly scary sound of thousands and thousands of dragons, in pursuit.

The Red-Rage sound in itself had to be fought, for it numbed the brain into defeat and despair.

"HUNT the HUMAN from the SKY
Burn him UP and let him Die
Hunt the human, hunt the human,"

'Don't listen,' sobbed Hiccup. 'Don't listen, Windwalker, don't listen...'

He made the mistake of glancing over his shoulder once and the sight was so terrifying it made his stomach turn to water. Thousands and thousands of dragons, murder in their eyes, the flames so close they were nearly touching him, a flying pack of ravenous and angry wolves, they'd tear him to pieces when they caught him.

The Red-Rage was getting closer, Hiccup could hear it, louder, louder, always louder.

"Give up..."

the Red-Rage was telling him, and Hiccup tried to close his brain but the noise seeped in anyway.

"You've lost already, Death is sweet, embrace it..."

The triumphant voice of the Dragon Furious.

"We've got him! We've GOT him!!"

The extraordinary, crazy, rock formations of the Gorge turned it into a gigantic slalom course. One second's lack of concentration and they would crash straight into a pillar of stone and knock themselves out of this world and into the next.

On top of this, the Gorge itself was shaped, as its name suggests, like a lightning bolt, and the cliffs twisted and turned around corners in a wildly contorted fashion.

Wooah, this needed advanced flying skills of the most extreme kind, super-extreme-advanced in fact, and if Gobber could have seen Hiccup picking his way through that Gorge like threading a needle at supersonic speed he would have been a very proud six-and-a-half-foot lunatic, very proud indeed.

'Toothless feel s-s-sick, slow down!' The little dragon popped his head out of Hiccup's shirt, screamed at the sight of an upcoming wall of stone that Hiccup steered the Windwalker wildly away from it right at the last minute, and dived down the shirt beside the Wodensfang again, putting his wings over his eyes for good measure.

OK, they weren't going to be able to out-run the pursuing dragons this way...

So he'd have to go UP instead.

'Up, Windwalker, up...'

The boy and the dragon shot up out of the Gorge like a firework, the swarm of dragons even closer now.

Hiccup urged the Windwalker higher and higher.

If we get high enough, a lot of them won't be able to follow, thought Hiccup.

You see, Hiccup's short life spent studying dragons meant that he knew so much about them. Most dragons much prefer operating in what they call 'shallow air'. The air close to the land, just out of reach of the tree-tops, is their environment and their playground. Very few dragons are 'deep air' dragons, they don't like the higher air above the clouds, with its sudden winds, and lighter atmosphere. They don't like that at all.

'Toothless's ears are p-p-popping!' wailed Toothless's muffled voice from deep in Hiccup's shirt, 'and he's s-s-squashed!'

'Higher, Windwalker, higher,' Hiccup whispered to the Windwalker.

He couldn't really breathe now. He tried not to think about what might happen if he passed out, because he wasn't tied on... Just a little higher...

The Windwalker's wings swam ever upwards. UP, UP, UP...

Hiccup's ears were popping too... but as he looked down, the dragons following them were fading in their pursuit. The Windwalker's wings were taking them further than they could follow.

The beautiful black dragon sailed on and on through the clouds, higher and higher, further and further.

The air was cold now... They were so high, leaving all of Hiccup's problems behind... Hiccup was extremely tired... He laid his face down on the Windwalker's back, and he slept.

He woke up in a cave he did not recognize.

What could he do now?

Even his helmet was lost.

It was a small thing but it made him feel so naked.

Hiccup's hair stood up like a hedgehog's, caked with dirt, the ends singed with flame. Without the helmet to cover it, the Slavemark blazed, a scar of shame on his forehead. His face grey with ash and streaked with tears.

'I am alone,' said Hiccup aloud. 'And far away.'

'You are not alone,' replied the Wodensfang gravely, sitting like a little statue guarding him a couple of feet away. 'You have these two dragons. And you have me.'

The Windwalker was sleeping in that alien cave, his long untidy body stretched out as peacefully as if he was snoozing on the cliff-face, as he snored, 'Hong... shuh,' dreaming once again of butterflies.

I am
a RUNT.

Toothless was awake and scratching himself and wondering what was for supper.

Hiccup hid his face in his elbow, for he was ashamed. 'Why are you helping me? I broke my promise to you, the instant that I made it...'

'You did not break your promise,' said the Wodensfang. 'You promised that you would try to do your best, and that is what you did. And I am helping you because you are not alone. For some reason these two very ordinary dragons—'

'Here, I s-s-say!' protested Toothless. 'Toothless not ordinary!'

'These two *exceptionally* common dragons,' continued the Wodensfang, 'have not succumbed to the Red-Rage. They have stayed loyal to you. There have been very few human beings throughout history who have created that kind of loyalty.'

The Wodensfang sighed.

His eyes looked back into the past. 'Humans have disappointed me, oh, so many times. Perhaps I am wrong, Hiccup the Third, but I think that you are different. You are the One. And for you, I'll hope again... just one last time...' There was such an ache in the old dragon's voice.

Hiccup's face was still in his elbow.

You see, this was a test, just like all the others. And perhaps it was the best test of all.

A Hero cannot triumph *all* the time.

Sometimes he will be defeated, and how he faces that defeat is a test of his character.

Flasburn had been given that test, late in his life, and he had been found wanting.

And now Hiccup Horrendous Haddock the Third had been defeated, perhaps even more thoroughly than Flashburn himself.

He had lost everything,

Tribe, friends, father, family. He was unarmed, in rags, alone and hiding in a cave. An Outcast and an exile.

For a while Hiccup cried into his elbow.

And then slowly, slowly, slowly, Hiccup Horrendous Haddock the Third brought down his arm.

He wiped his nose with the end of his sleeve. And...

'I'll try not to let you down,' said Hiccup the Third. 'What can I do?'

'You can find the Dragon Jewel,' said the

Wodensfang. 'The Jewel is the only thing the Dragon Furious will listen to now. He is afraid of it. I am afraid of it myself. For if it is broken, the Jewel has the power to destroy dragons for ever...'

'Where is this Jewel hidden?' asked Hiccup.

'The Jewel disappeared, like all the King's Things, when Grimbeard the Ghastly died,' replied the Wodensfang. 'But it is said that the Dragonsword holds the secret of where the Jewel is now.'

'Old Wrinkly said "the sword points the way",' said Hiccup. 'But I don't have the sword any more. Alvin the Treacherous has the sword.'

The Wodensfang sighed. 'This is true,' he said sadly. 'And this makes it even more important that we should get hold of the Jewel first. After only a very short acquaintance I can see that this Alvin the Treacherous is an extremely unpleasant human being. If he finds the Jewel he will not hesitate to use it, and dragons shall be no more.'

Gloom settled on the already-gloomy little cave.

Toothless was bored of all this talking, and aware that everybody had got their priorities completely wrong and weren't really caring about the more vital question of what Toothless was going to eat next.

He was getting sleepy again, so he climbed on to Hiccup's shoulder, took Hiccup's face between his paws so that Hiccup had to look at him straight in the eyes, and said: 'M-m-master. Tell this old brown d-d-dragon that this waistcoat is T-T-TOOTHLESS'S place. Because *Toothless* is Hiccup's h-h-hunting-dragon.'

'Of course you are, Toothless,' said Hiccup, stroking Toothless behind the ears. 'There's only one dragon for me.'

Satisfied, Toothless burrowed down Hiccup's waistcoat again, and as he wriggled around trying to get comfy in his special place right above Hiccup's heart, the waistcoat rustled, reminding Hiccup of something.

A great surge of hope rose within him... Surely it wasn't possible?

'Wodensfang,' said Hiccup eagerly. 'How does the sword show the way to the Jewel?'

'You're a clever boy, Hiccup,' said the Wodensfang. 'You must know that it is not the sword itself that is important. The Dragonsword, or, what did you call it? The Endeavour, is a perfectly ordinary sword, more ordinary than most. What is important is not the sword itself, but what is *inside* the sword. There is a secret compartment—'

'Yes, yes, I know!' said Hiccup impatiently. 'I found that ages ago! And inside the secret compartment is – *this...* '

Hiccup reached into his waistcoat and took out the paper that was Grimbeard the Ghastly's Last Will and Testament. He had shoved it into his waistcoat a couple of weeks ago when Stoick shouted at him from the Battle Arena, and he had completely forgotten to put it back in the secret compartment again.

The Wodensfang looked at him open-mouthed. 'Well, bless my wings and whiskers!'

'I took it out earlier and forgot to put it back,' explained Hiccup.

'Grimbeard's map to show where the Jewel is hidden!' exclaimed the Wodensfang, in delight.

'But it isn't a map,' said Hiccup. Typical Grimbeard to make things even more difficult than they already were. 'It's Grimbeard's will.'

Hiccup read it aloud:

I leave to my True Heir, this my favourite sword.

Because the Stormblade always lunged a little to the left.

And the Best is not always the most
Obvious.

Yours,

In the hope that you will make a better
Leader than I was,

G.G.

Hiccup's hands were still stained purple
with Vorpent venom, from wrestling with
the witch. And as he read, the venom
seemed to be doing something to the paper.
Hiccup was about to wipe them, when to his
astonishment, he realized that words were
appearing. The purple was bringing out a
secret message, a message that had not been
seen for over one hundred years.

Courage
(said the message)

What is within is more important than
what is without.

This is not The End, I promise.

Here is the map.

And the map can lead you to the
Dragon Jewel.

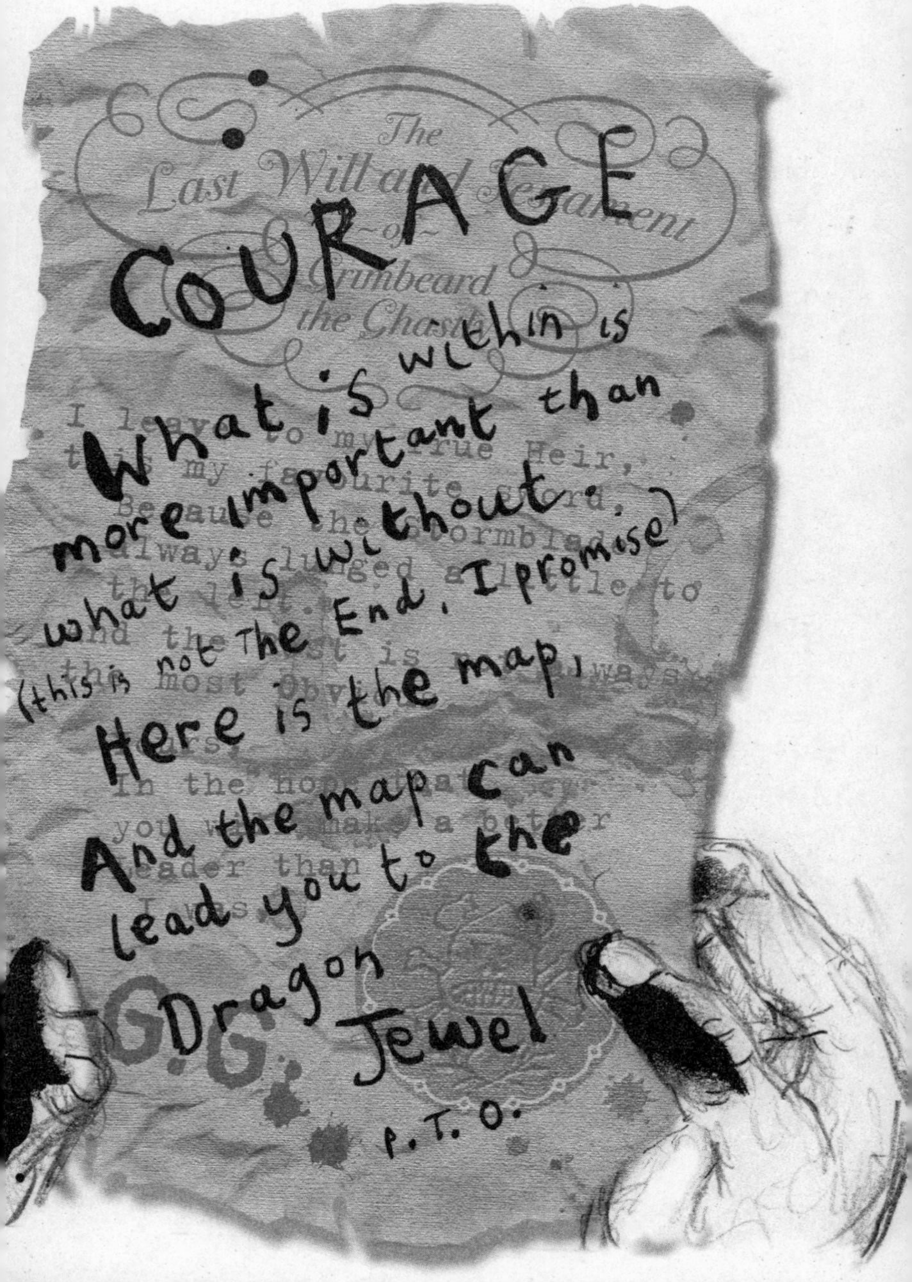

COURAGE

The Last Will and Testament ~of~ Grimbeard the Ghastly

*I leave to my True Heir,
this, my favourite Sword,
Because the Stormblade
always plunged a little to
the left...*

What is within is more important than what is without.

(this is not The End, I promise)

Here is the map

And the map can lead you to the

Dragon Jewel

P.T.O.

G.G.

Hiccup turned the piece of paper over. It was blank on the other side, but as he rubbed it with the Vorpent venom, lines began to appear.

The lines of a map. A map that would lead him to the Dragon Jewel. The Rebellion COULD be stopped after all.

The boy leapt to his feet.

'This is not the End!' he shouted.

This is not 'THE END!'

Far, far away, there was another shout.

Half burnt, their sails dark with fire, the Viking
navy limped out of the Eastern Archipelago, singing
the song of the Dead. The Vikings were barbarians,
but their voices were very beautiful.

> 'Turn their bones to coral, Thor,
> Their song to wind and hearts to gold,
> They'll live for ever in the skies,
> Eating rainbows with the gods.'

And then the song turning darker, the rhythmic drums
threatening:

> 'Give us now our just revenge,
> Instead of corn now bring us blood,

Turn our peacetime into war,
Let us feast on knives and swords.'

To the angry beat of this song came the ominous sound of swords being sharpened, axes banged on shields.

Way at the front of the snaking line of ships, were the Outcast vessels.

Once the pariahs of the Archipelago, now its leaders.

On the very first ship, the witch Excellinor and her son, the new King of the Wilderwest.

'Let me show you, Alvin, dearest,' cooed the witch, 'the secret of the Dragonsword…'

Cloak flapping round her in the wind like a malevolent bat, greedy bony fingers fingering the

sword's secret compartment.

A shriek, as the witch Excellinor opened up the secret compartment of the sword, and found that it was empty.

A terrible, disappointed howl. 'That wretched burglaring little rat has stolen the map!'

No, this was

NOT THE END

I'm going to GET you
Hiccup Horrendous Haddock III,
if it's the last thing I do!!

EPILOGUE by Cressida Cowell, translator of the Hiccup memoirs

When I was a little girl, living on an island in a deep blue sea, I asked myself a question.

'What if dragons really existed?'

So imagine my excitement when I was the first one to translate the first of Hiccup's memoirs, and I realized, trembling, that the frail nearly-not-there writing on the document was answering that simple glorious question for the very first time.

A question that humans had asked themselves across the vastness of continents, across the inky span of centuries, here finally found, in one tiny box, discovered one accidental day by a boy on a beach. Here, at last, was the answer!

Dragons DID exist. And this was the proof.

Now I am on to the ninth of his memoirs, and I know there is not long to go.

But what I am realizing, slowly, gradually, is that the memoirs are asking a question to which I do not really want to know the answer.

If dragons really existed, what happened to the dragons? Where are they now?

I dread to know the answer to this question. I do not want to know. Because I have an awful feeling that Hiccup, whom I have grown to love, has something to do with their disappearance.

I do not want to know, and if I had known that this was the question in the first place, perhaps I would not have started. But I cannot stop now...

I have to know the answer.

THE
REBELLION
HAS
BEGUN

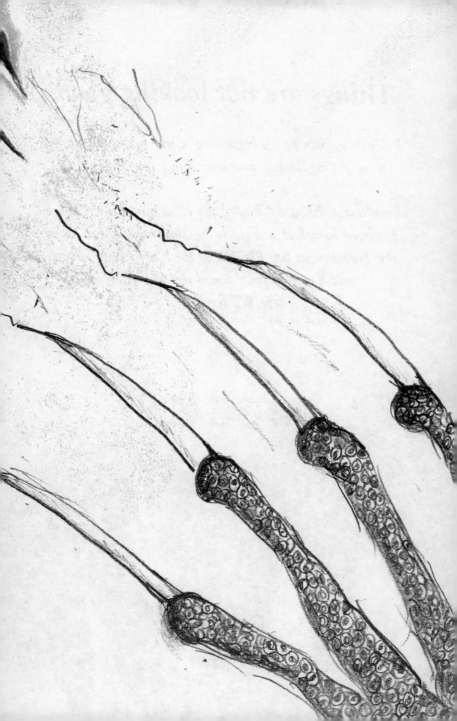

Things are not looking good.

I told you, right at the beginning of this book, that things were getting darker, and now things are darker still.

Snotlout is the new Chief of the Hooligan Tribe. Stoick has been banished and given the Slavemark. And Alvin the Treacherous has **EIGHT** *of the King's Lost Things, and has been proclaimed the new King of the Wilderwest…*

What can Hiccup do, alone as he is, and hunted now by both humans and dragons alike?
Can he find the Dragon Jewel, mankind's last and only hope? And if he does, what will he do with it?

Watch out for the next volume
of Hiccup's memoirs...

HOW THE HOOK
SURVIVED THE FLAMES

Things were so hectic there, that I didn't get a moment to describe to you how Alvin and his mother survived the fire on Berserk.

At the end of *How to Break a Dragon's Heart*, Alvin plunged into the heart of the inferno, and his mother, the Witch Excellinor, jumped down after him. By some horrible miracle, they fell down into the only lake on Berserk, and although they are evil, you have to admire their resilience. They swam around in circles for nearly two days (a remarkable feat for an elderly woman and a one-legged, one-armed man) before the fire burnt itself out. Then they picked their way across the smoking remains of the island, and the witch's powers of persuasion managed to hitch them a lift with a passing Visithug ship to the Outcast Lands.

I cannot tell you, however, how the witch managed to kidnap UG the Uglithug along the way.

I know some of the witch's secrets, but not all.

This is Cressida, age 9, writing on the island.

Cressida Cowell grew up in London and
on a small, uninhabited island off the west
coast of Scotland where she spent her time
writing stories, fishing for things to eat,
and exploring the island looking for dragons.
She was convinced that there were dragons
living on the island, and has been
fascinated by them ever since.

www.cressidacowell.com

HOWDEEDOODEETHERE!

For your latest news on all things dragon and Cressida Cowell please follow:

 @cressidacowellauthor

 @cressidacowell

 facebook.com/
cressidacowellauthor

 Toodleoon for now...

'Cowell's How to Train Your Dragon
books are national treasures.'
Amanda Craig, *The Times*

'Bound to become a modern classic.'
Independent

'Always thrilling, funny and brilliantly
illustrated.' ***Daily Express***

'Cressida Cowell is a splendid story-teller
... young readers are lucky to have her.'
Books for Keeps

'One of the greatest inventions
of modern children's literature.'
Julia Eccleshare, LoverReading4kids

'Funny, outrageous and will lure in the
most reluctant reader.' ***Spectator***

'As with the best children's literature, these books
are about much bigger things: endurance,
loyalty, friendship and love.' ***Daily Telegraph***

'Cowell's loopy scattershot imagination is
as compelling as ever.' ***Financial Times***

CRESSIDA COWELL
HOW TO TRAIN YOUR
DRAGON

AUDIO
Read by
DAVID
TENNANT

LOOK OUT FOR
CRESSIDA COWELL'
NEW SERIES

the
Wizards
of
ONCE

Once there
was Magic...

This is the story of a young boy Wizard, and a
young girl Warrior, who have been taught to
hate each other like poison.

#wizardsofonce